D1742891

Charming Memory

EL Bossert

Published by Two Boots Publishing, 2018.

CHARMING MEMORY

First edition. May 25, 2018.

Written by EL Bossert.

For Brett

Chapter One

AS SHE FINISHED THE first of her Saturday morning errands, Jamie chatted amicably with the hardware store clerk. She heard her cell phone whistle, indicating a call from her fifteen-year-old nephew, Marco. He was in charge of watching Max, her four-year-old son, at the playground by the library just a few blocks away.

Jamie had barely lifted the phone to her ear when she heard the desperation in Marco's voice, "I lost him!"

Abandoning her purchase, Jamie ran out the door into the street. From the direction of the playground, she heard a woman's scream followed by tires screeching. More yelling punctuated the air. Jamie took off in a dead sprint toward the spot where she last saw Max.

· · · ·

THE MORNING HAD BEGUN as a typical early summer day. Jamie quietly entered her son's room and lifted the window blind, allowing the morning sun to illuminate the room. Max stirred slightly, turning his face away from the light. Jamie still marveled at how this small person completely captured her heart. Some people went on and on about how *brave* she was, being a single parent. But most days, Jamie did not feel brave at all. She was more likely to feel a mixture of joy, intense responsibility, and gratitude. Also, she did not feel like a single parent as she had surrounded herself and Max with a family of kin and close friends.

Jamie sat on the edge of Max's bed and leaned over to plant a gentle kiss on his cheek.

"Time to wake up, mijo," Jamie spoke softly into his ear.

Max moaned as his eyes opened and he graced his mother with a morning grin.

"Come on, put these clothes on. We're going into town this morning." Jamie gently tousled Max's soft brown hair as he climbed out of bed and changed from pajamas to the shorts and t-shirt she offered. He followed her to the kitchen where breakfast was already on the table.

After breakfast, Jamie buckled Max into his car seat and drove the half-mile lane to her sister's house to pick up Marco. The road to Crestwood was quiet on this bright morning in late May. The sun was shining but the smell of fresh rain from the night before hung in the air.

Crestwood is a small, quaint town, at the crossroads of two state highways, far from any interstate freeway. There are no big factories nor is it a tourist destination. A few small wineries and farms specializing in artisan foods dot the landscape around town. There is the beauty of rolling hills and woodlands, but nothing extraordinary. Only the locals fish and boat on the nearby small lake. A much larger lake several miles south of town draws people from the region seeking recreation, but no one has to drive through Crestwood to get there. Crestwood is not exactly in the middle of nowhere, but a non-local did not arrive by accident.

As Jamie turned onto Main Street, heading toward downtown, she saw a tall, smartly handsome woman she did not recognize walking along the sidewalk. The woman carried a large camping backpack. *That's odd*, Jamie thought to herself, *Crestwood is not a typical hiking destination*. Her thought was interrupted by Max, asking questions about where they were going.

Jamie parked by the city library. She walked toward the hardware store down the street while Max ran to the playground beside the library, opened the gate in the fence, and let himself in. Marco dutifully followed close behind.

"Go play," Marco mindlessly ordered Max. Marco took a seat on a bench, absorbed in videos and text chatting with a few friends who were also involuntarily awake at this early hour of the day.

A dozen other children were already playing on swings and slides as their parents stood talking to each other on the side of the playground. Max, inconspicuous in his red shorts and white T-shirt, quietly observed his surroundings from his perch atop a bouncing green crocodile. His short, straight brown hair was a few shades darker than his smooth skin. No one paid any particular attention to him.

As Max took in his surroundings, a large, gray tabby cat lying just outside the playground fence caught his attention. Moving quietly in the direction of the cat, Max slipped unnoticed out of the playground gate. Instead of yelling *kitty* or *gatito* as most children his age would, Max stealthily made his way toward the cat. The first brush of a hand across her fur startled the cat, causing her to bolt across the street. Max followed.

Cars parked on both sides of the one-way street allowed for a single lane of traffic. Emerging from between two parked cars, Max stood in the middle of the street looking for the cat. He walked along, bending over to check under each car.

From the playground bench, Marco looked up from his phone, scanning for his cousin. Panic spread across his face when he realized Max was no longer in sight. Marco rushed over to the group of parents talking amongst themselves on the far side of the playground.

"Has anyone seen Max?" Marco's voice was urgent as he continued scanning the playground.

The parents shook their heads *no* and began to look around as Marco dialed his aunt's phone number.

"I lost him!"

• • • •

IN THE STREET, MAX stood still for a moment. A scream distracted him. He looked around to see where the sound came from. Suddenly an arm around his waist lifted him off the ground and he felt himself flying through the air. A loud thud and crack was followed by more screaming.

Max felt his body encased, tightly held to someone's chest by arms wrapped around him. A hot surge of pain in his hand caused him to wince. Max wiggled his head free to look at the person holding him. Glazed eyes framed by closely cropped waves of dark brown hair barely focused on him. The woman attempted to speak but no sound emerged. Blood matted her hair on one side and dripped slowly down the sharply defined face.

"Boo-boo." Max freed one arm and pointed at the stranger's face,

"Boo—," the stranger's eyes abruptly closed and her body went limp.

Hearing the screams, Marco had run to the street. He saw his cousin lying on top of a stranger on the hood of a car. He reached for Max but the child held onto the stranger repeating, *boo-boo*. Other people tried to calm the child and assess the injuries to both Max and his rescuer. One of the parents from the playground called 911.

"Max! MAX!" Jamie pushed her way through the gathered people.

Max refused to release his hold on the stranger, shaking his head *no* to his mother's tug. He pointed at the trickle of blood on the stranger's face, "Boo-boo."

"Does it hurt anywhere?" Jamie deliberately calmed her voice.

"My arm hurts." Max's eyes brimmed with tears.

Wanting more than anything to hold her child close, but uncertain of the extent of Max's injuries, Jamie allowed him to remain on top of the stranger. She laid her head against his back gently, tears filling her eyes.

Within a couple of minutes, two city police cars, a sheriff's deputy's vehicle, a fire truck, and an ambulance filled the street. It took two paramedics and a calm, deep-voiced firefighter to convince Max to release his grip on the stranger. As they lifted Max away from the limp body of his rescuer, they discovered two of his fingers brightly swollen and possibly broken. Two paramedics loaded Max into the ambulance for further examination as the others turned their attention to the unconscious stranger.

The driver of the truck that almost hit Max concentrated as he answered the questions of one of the police officers. He spoke slowly, as if reconstructing every detail in his mind.

"I came around the corner and flipped my visor down. The sun was in my eyes and the glare off the wet street blinded me. All of a sudden, out of nowhere, I saw something flying in front of me. There was a loud sound, *thud*. I stopped as quick as I could and got out to look. This woman was screaming and running toward me. I swear I didn't see anyone. I would never hurt a kid. I was being careful." The driver shook uncontrollably, slumping against his truck as the officer scribbled notes.

A second officer queried the group of people standing nearby to find out if anyone had witnessed the incident. Two people raised their hands. The others had only seen the aftermath, not the actual event. The officer took statements from the witnesses first, then the others. The woman who had screamed offered her account.

"I was putting a bag in my car, the blue one," she explained, pointing twenty yards down the street. "I looked up to check for traffic and saw the kid in the middle of the street and a big truck coming right at him. The truck wasn't slowing down, so I screamed. I was sure the poor child was about to get hit when this person comes out of nowhere. She grabbed the kid and jumped. You could tell she was trying to protect the kid. Somehow twisted herself and landed on her back, not on him. I've never seen anything like it."

The second witness provided a similar story.

"I saw someone swoop in and grab the kid. The truck hit her leg and kind of knocked her around. I heard a loud bang when she landed on the car. I ran over, trying to not get hit myself. I don't think the truck driver could see a thing."

The officer asked the gathered group if anyone knew the identity of the rescuer the paramedics were attending to. Each person shook their head *no*. Someone offered, *a freakin' hero, that's who*. They all nodded, murmuring their agreement.

Someone who had not witnessed the accident itself, came forward claiming to have passed the *hero* on the sidewalk just before the incident.

"She had a big backpack," the witness told the police officer, "I think it was black. When I heard a woman yelling, I came around the corner over there and ran over to see if I could help. I don't see the backpack anywhere."

The officers continued taking statements and initiated a search of the area for the backpack.

In the nearby ambulance, Jamie sat next to Max. She held him cautiously. Max was quiet, his alert brown eyes studiously watching as his mother answered questions from a police officer and a paramedic simultaneously.

"No, he doesn't have any drug allergies that we know of."

"I was down the street at the hardware store."

"Marco was watching him."

"That's his cousin standing right there."

Jamie turned her attention to Marco, who was shifting uncomfortably from foot-to-foot at the end of the ambulance, looking unsure of what to do next. Speaking in a measured tone to conceal her anger and fear, Jamie issued a clear order.

"Call your mom and dad to pick you up at the library and meet us at the hospital."

Marco nodded, the shame of losing his cousin pulling his shoulders down into a hunch.

The doors of the ambulance were closed and the driver navigated the narrow space to leave for the hospital.

Meanwhile, two paramedics talked over each other as they assessed the condition of the *hero*.

"Pulse, slow but steady."

"Pupils, responsive but sluggish."

"Looks like a nasty gash on the side of the head." The blood was traced back to its source and pressure applied.

A neck brace was slipped on to stabilize the patient's head and neck. Two firefighters helped straighten out the rest of the woman's body, carefully checking for any obvious broken bones. A large bruise was forming on her elbow and arm, most likely from hitting the car hood. The eyes of the patient flew open when her ankle was moved.

"Pain recoil. That's a good sign," one paramedic noted.

A spinal board was slipped under the patient's body to stabilize her for transport. The first ambulance transporting Max and his mother had rolled away as soon as the second ambulance appeared. Paramedics and firefighters loaded the morning's hero in the back and raced off to the nearby ER.

"Marco," Marco's father, Bryan, called out as he arrived at the scene, "what happened?" Bryan could see the regretful tears in Marco's eyes, so he held back his anger. There would be time later to decide on the consequences for this act of negligence.

Seeing that Marco's father had arrived, a police officer approached to take Marco's statement.

"I was sitting on the bench over there," Marco explained, "I was on my phone. I thought Max would just play with the other kids. I didn't see him leave. I heard some woman scream and ran out here."

"You're lucky someone was paying attention and saved him." The police officer frowned deeply, shaking his head.

By the end of the preliminary investigation, a story had emerged. A child, alone in the street, was saved from certain death by an unnamed hero. The hero cracked her head on the windshield of a car and was still unconscious. No one recognized her, and the backpack that most likely held her identity was nowhere to be found.

Chapter Two

ON THE SHORT RIDE TO the hospital, Jamie alternated tears of relief that Max appeared to be barely harmed with anger at Marco for losing Max. Then she wallowed in feeling like a bad mother for leaving her only child at a playground while she ran seemingly inconsequential errands. For a brief moment, Jamie wished she had a partner, someone to co-parent Max with, to share this trauma.

Jamie wore what she liked to call her Saturday morning sweats. The loose light gray sweatpants and sky blue sweatshirt did little to obscure her toned body. Her dark auburn brown hair was shoulder length, pulled back carelessly behind her ears into a short ponytail. The Italian-Welsh features of her face were dark and ambiguous enough that many people had a difficult time discerning her ancestry, a big plus in her line of work. It was her blue-green eyes that showed the weight of the morning's trauma.

Jamie's sister, Sarah, nearly beat the ambulance carrying Max and Jamie to the ER, breaking several traffic laws on her way. When she arrived at the hospital the nurses were wheeling Max into the ER with Jamie practically on the stretcher beside him. Sarah rushed to her sister's side.

It was obvious to even the most casual observer that Sarah was Jamie's sister. Her facial features were carved from the same block, even though her pinker skin tone and russet colored hair favored their father's side of the family.

"He'll be okay," Sarah held Jamie's hand as they watched as the doctors examined every inch of Max's small body.

The doctors did not detect any bruising beyond Max's hand nor did he flinch when they touched or moved any other part of his body. Amazingly, Max seemed to have only a couple of broken fingers. The trip to the x-ray room was more traumatic for Jamie and Sarah than Max himself.

"The fractures to Max's fingers are minor and will not require surgery," a pediatric resident assured Jamie as he taped the fingers together and put a splint on the hand. "We want Max to stay overnight at the hospital, so we can keep an eye on him, just in case we missed anything. We'll give him something for the swelling in his hand to relieve the pain. The nurse will be in soon."

After Max was moved into a private room, a nurse came in with children's pain reliever for Max, who slurped down the cherry red liquid without complaint.

"Where's Boo?" Max inquired before he fell asleep in Jamie's arms.

"Who's Boo?" Sarah asked Jamie.

"I think it may be the person who saved him. When I found him, he was pointing at her head and saying boo-boo. He wouldn't let go of her. Then he asked in the ambulance several times and was really concerned that Boo was not in the ambulance with us."

"Do you know what happened to her?"

"No. I need to find her. I need to thank her. I asked one of the paramedics but she couldn't tell me anything. Said something about they didn't have a name yet."

"I'll ask the nurses. They probably can't tell me anything about her condition, but maybe I can at least find out her name, talk to her family or something. I saw another ambulance come in while we were in the ER. That must have been her." Sarah walked out of the room on her mission, leaving a sleeping Max in Jamie's arms.

• • • •

THE SECOND AMBULANCE carrying Max's still unconscious savior rolled into the ER twenty minutes after the first. A story about the incoming patient, who valiantly saved a small child from certain death, had already circulated the unit. The ER nurse in charge labeled the chart *Hero Doe*.

"Chart? Signs?" a doctor barked as the medical team moved quickly and efficiently around the prone figure. The rest of Hero Doe's clothes were cut away and handed to a police officer to search for any information or clues about her identity. A quick buzz cut of the patient's hair allowed closer examination of the head wound.

"Brain may swell. Hook up the EEG," the doctor ordered.

A nurse attached wires to the patient's skull to monitor brain activity. The patient's eyes fluttered open and closed a couples of times. Her limbs twitched, but she did not respond to verbal commands.

"Get a neurologist in here," the doctor called out. "We need a consult immediately. Order a CAT scan ASAP to check for skull fractures."

The patient stirred again, opening her eyes wider this time.

"Can you feel me touching your hand?" a nurse asked.

No response.

"Can you move your finger for me?"

A slight movement in the patient's index finger. The nurse was pleased and continued to make requests. The patient moved each leg no more than an inch then let out a low moan. The patient closed her eyes.

A second doctor joined the team, leading a discussion about whether the patient was stable enough for the CAT scan or even an x-ray of her skull.

Hearing the discussion around her, the patient became aware she was in a hospital. The intense ache in her head pounded every time someone spoke. There were several references to *Hero Doe*, but that made no sense to her. Drifting in and out of consciousness slowly gave way to a more awakened state.

"Can you tell us your name?" the doctor asked.

The patient tried to shake her head but something prevented her head from moving. She groaned *no* instead.

"Do you know what day it is?"

Another groan.

A series of questions finally led to a halting answer from the patient.

"Hospital...no where...no why...no name."

"You are in the hospital in Crestwood," the nurse spoke directly and clearly. "You hit your head on a car windshield and have been unconscious for about an hour. You saved a little boy. We don't know your name yet."

"Oh," was all the patient could manage while trying to process this new information. Finally, she asked, "How's kid?"

"He'll be fine, we think he just has a couple of broken fingers," the nurse responded, even though it was a minor privacy violation. However, under the circumstances, the patient most likely would not remember two minutes later anyway. "How are you feeling? Can you tell us if you hurt somewhere?"

The patient contemplated for a moment before replying with a list, "Head...leg...arm...my name?"

"Hero Doe. For now."

"Oh." The patient closed her eyes and drifted off to sleep.

• • • •

SARAH FOUND A COUPLE of nurses at the station outside Max's room and inquired about the person who saved Max. One of the nurses told her they could not release information to a non-family member, then added they had not heard anything anyway. Sarah made her way to the ER to ask the intake clerk. She received the same answer initially. Then, without looking up, the clerk mumbled as if talking to himself, *no family has arrived for that patient.*

Sarah walked back to Max's room, passing the main entrance to the hospital. She could see a few reporters already gathered outside. A police officer tried to keep them to one side to prevent interference with people who actually needed to be at the hospital.

"A couple of hours and the vultures are already here." Sarah barely disguised her disgust as she relayed the scene to Jamie along with the lack of information about the woman who saved Max.

"I saw Dani when I was in the ambulance with Max. She was respectful, but clearly she had to put something online. Didn't take long," Jamie replied.

Jamie knew Dani, a reporter, socially. They went on one date shortly after Dani moved to Crestwood to work at the local newspaper. Within ten minutes they realized they were best suited for a professional relationship, not a personal one. Jamie gave Dani a couple of exclusive interviews over the years as a courtesy, to support Dani's career. In return, Dani respected Jamie's privacy, but she couldn't do anything about the other reporters. That was the closest Jamie ever came to a healthy relationship with a reporter.

"What do you want me to do? I can make a statement for the family? Ask for privacy, that sort of thing?" Sarah was prepared to take on the duty of family spokesperson to protect her sister and nephew.

"That would be good. The hospital will try to protect us. Is anyone else here?" Jamie asked.

"Bryan and Marco and Gee. They're hanging out in the café. Shon went to the house to pack up a few things and is on the way. I haven't reached Mom and Dad yet."

"Draft something up, please. Just say Max is doing well and we would like privacy."

The press conference started mid-afternoon. The head of hospital administration gave a brief statement first.

"We can confirm that two people arrived at the trauma unit. We cannot comment on the condition of either patient or release their identity, but Sarah Jordan-Dirk will make a statement."

Sarah stepped up to the podium of microphones in a small meeting room.

"I would like to confirm that my nephew, Max Jordan, was brought to the hospital this morning after a minor accident. He has a couple of broken fingers. The doctors and staff in the ER provided excellent treatment. Max is resting comfortably and will be fine. His mother, Jamie Jordan, is with him. We ask that you all respect our privacy, as well as the privacy of other patients and their families. We appreciate the concern that has been extended to Max, his mother, and our family. Thank you."

Reporters yelled a cacophony of questions at anyone who might answer. *Who is the second person? Is it true that your son, Marco, was involved in the accident? Was Max killed by a truck? What is the condition of the second person?*

"We have no additional information for you at this time." The hospital administrator put an end to the press conference and asked security to clear the room and entryway.

As they retreated into the hospital corridor, Sarah apologized to the administrator for the inconvenience to the hospital, who shook her head and sighed.

"We'll try to keep them outside. I'll ask for security at Max's door, but that will just tip them off it's his room. If everything goes well you can all be out of here early tomorrow." The administrator then added, "This was the first time I could honestly say I have no further information. We still don't have a clue who this hero is."

The conversation was cut short by the appearance of the County Sheriff. The sheriff was a long-time friend of the Jordan family. She earned the nickname Chief one night when, ignoring a bleeding wound from a bullet that had grazed her arm during a chase, took down and arrested a man who had committed an armed robbery. One of the officers on the scene started to exclaim, *you the man*, but stopped himself and changed it to, *you the Chief*. The new title stuck.

"Sorry to bother you, Sarah, but I need to show you a picture and see if you recognize this person." Chief held up a photo printed on a sheet of paper.

The person in the head shot was not immediately identifiable as female or male, with eyes closed and gauze obscuring the forehead.

"No, I don't recognize...is this our hero?" Sarah shivered, "Is she dead?"

"No, she's not dead," Chief replied. "We took the picture before she was conscious. We are trying to get an ID. It's my understanding she is conscious now but can't remember her name or anything about the incident. None of the witnesses at the scene recognized her. I wanted to show this to you and Jamie and the family to find out if any of you recall seeing her before. Do you think Jamie is up for taking a look?"

If anyone else had asked, Sarah would have put them off, but Jamie and Chief had been close friends since high school. Chief was almost as protective of Jamie as Sarah herself was. This was probably the reason why Chief was taking on such a mundane task.

"Yes, I'm sure she will want to help out if she can. Max has already asked about Boo. That's the name he gave our hero." Sarah led the way to Max's room. "Do you think Max had some contact with this person before? Like someone tried to grab him?"

"Not from the reports I've heard, but we will be checking into everything. It will help when we have her real name."

Chief and Sarah arrived in Max's room, finding him groggy from the pain medicine and quietly playing with a puzzle using his un-splinted hand while Jamie watched and spoke softly to comfort him, and herself. Seeing Chief, Jamie rose from the bedside to embrace her friend. Max held his arms up for a hug, too.

"I am very happy to see you, tiger." Chief smiled at Max affectionately, enfolding the child in her arms gently and tousling his hair. Chief held out the picture to Jamie, shielding the eerie portrait from Max's view. "Sorry to bother you but have you ever seen this person before?"

Jamie studied the picture for a moment. The purple T-shirt tipped her off that this was the person on the hood of the car who had saved Max. At the scene, she had briefly looked at the blood streaked face and wondered if it was the woman she had seen walking down the sidewalk.

"Not before this morning. I saw her lying on the car, and I think it might be the same person I saw walking down Main Street as we came into town, but that woman had a big backpack. Is she okay?"

"They are still assessing her condition," Chief replied. "We should take another picture now that she's opened her eyes. She doesn't appear to be local. She can't remember her name, where she's from, or why she's in Crestwood. A witness said she had a backpack, but it's missing. We think someone picked it up. There are a couple of homeless guys, regulars on that street, we are looking for them. I know you see a lot of people. We thought you might remember meeting her somewhere else. When you were off on location or something."

"No, nothing comes to mind." Jamie looked at the picture again, studying the sharp facial features. "Will she be okay? I need to thank her."

"They said her condition is fair but stable. We're canvassing the stores in the area for surveillance tapes to see if she's on them somewhere. Something will turn up."

"You said she's awake. When can I see her? I want to make sure she receives whatever care she needs." Concern creased Jamie's face.

"I can't tell you a lot, but I will say she hit her head pretty darn hard. Cracked the windshield. A neurologist is coming in. The staff will be very thorough. The story about her saving Max has made the rounds. They said her memory should come back if there aren't any complications." What Chief did not add was that the process of recovering memories could take weeks, or months.

"Thanks Chief. Let me know if there's anything I can do." Jamie turned her attention back to Max.

Chapter Three

TWO DAYS AFTER HIS discharge, Jamie and Max returned to the hospital for a follow-up appointment. Jamie dropped by the inpatient wing where *Hero Doe* had been moved to see if she could shake lose any news about the injured woman.

"Boo!" Max yelled when he saw the tall woman stick her head out the door of the staff break room and took off toward her before Jamie could flinch.

"Max, stop," Jamie called as loudly as she thought she should in a hospital. "Max, no." She hurried to catch him, but he had a head start and no inhibition about reaching his target.

"Boo," Max reached his hero and leapt into her arms. Fortunately she avoided crunching his broken fingers as she caught him.

"Well...Max, it's good to see you! Oh my, what happened to your hand?"

"Remember, you saved me. Like Supergirl! You flew in and saved me from the truck!"

"I did?" the woman replied with equal enthusiasm. "Wow! But you hurt your hand."

"You broke it. But that's okay, you didn't mean to," Max offered matter-of-factly.

"I'm sorry. I'm glad you forgive me—what did you call me?"

"Boo!"

"Is that my name?"

"Yes!" Max pronounced.

Boo looked up to see Jamie and a nurse standing in front of her. Extending her free hand to Jamie, Boo politely introduced herself.

"You must be Max's mother? I'm...Boo. Sounds a lot less pretentious than Hero." Boo gave the nurse a humble look.

"Hi, I'm Jamie, and yes, I am Max's mother." Jamie cocked her head to one side to inquire, "They said you can't remember your name, but you remember Max?"

"No, not really," Boo turned her head slightly away from Max, who was running his un-splinted hand over her nearly bald head. "I heard you call him. He

14

seemed so excited to see me, I didn't want to spoil it." Boo lifted an eyebrow and shrugged.

Jamie was relieved to sense Boo did not recognize her. She had learned to pick up on the moment of awe when someone realizes they are meeting a celebrity. Boo seemed to have a pleasantly blank face when looking at her. The innocence was refreshing.

"How are you feeling?" Jamie took her first long look at Boo's face, studying the strong jaw, the lines forming at the sides of Boo's nearly golden light brown eyes, and the deep dimple on one side of the her face. Her unevenly shaved hair was still mostly obscured by gauze bandages. The bronzed skin of Boo's sinewy forearms and well-defined biceps suggested she spent a lot of time outdoors. Boo definitely had roguish good looks even if she was a little worse for wear at the moment. Jamie consciously forced herself to stop staring.

"I'm able to hobble around. Bit of a bruise on my ankle. Guess my big boots saved it from being broken. Otherwise, just minor bruises. Oh, yeah, a bit of a head-bang." Boo rolled her eyes toward the gash in her head, which had been stitched and taped over.

"I need to thank you for saving Max. They told me you grabbed him and..." Tears filled Jamie's eyes. "If it hadn't been for you..." Jamie couldn't finish that sentence either.

"Well, I am glad I did whatever I did, because this little person is precious." Boo gave the child in her arms a little tighter squeeze. "Hey, Max, if it's okay with your mother, do you want some ice cream? The nurses hide some in the freezer, but I think they'll share."

"Mom, can I?"

"Yes, go ahead, but not too much. It's almost lunchtime."

Boo silently thanked Jamie for her permission, then addressed the nurse.

"You can tell..." Boo paused to think, "Jamie—I'm not too good with re-membering names yet, but I'm getting better. You can tell Jamie what you told me about retro amnesia or whatever fancy name you called it. Right now this seems to be as close as I have to family."

As Boo and Max disappeared into the staff break room, the nurse eyed Jamie. There was no harm in sharing the basic information about the patient's condition.

"Boo, as she will now be known, has a mild to severe concussion. We are still monitoring her for any complications, seizures, brain swelling or other symptoms from her injury. There do not appear to be any other serious injuries. She has a bruised ankle, where the truck hit her, and bruises on her arm and hip, where she landed on the car. She has near-total loss of memory of names, places, and prior events in her life, but the basics are still there. We are following a concussion protocol, trying not to overstimulate her brain. But we're also trying to help her remember things if she can. This type of amnesia typically reverses and the patient recovers some or even most of their memory...eventually."

"I don't know what to say. Is there anything I can do?" Jamie asked.

"I don't think the police have turned up any ID yet. We'll keep her for at least a week and hope we make some progress. If she hasn't remembered her name, someone will have to decide where she goes. It's unclear what will happen at that point."

"Please let me know if there is anything I can do. I owe her everything." Tears stung Jamie's eyes again.

"This is the perkiest I've seen Boo since she came to our unit. I won't tell if you pop back in for a visit. Hanging out with nurses and doctors who just want to poke and ask you how many times you've had a bowel movement today gets rather boring. We have not turned on the TV or offered her access to the computer, and she hasn't asked. We are trying to limit stimulus. A little interaction might help. I'm sure you're busy and it's a lot to ask, but we have all rather taken a liking to Boo. She may not remember her name, but she remembers her manners. She is quite a charmer."

Jamie relaxed, feeling more at ease believing Boo did not recognize her. It was a long-lost sensation to meet someone with such a clean slate.

· · · ·

"HOW'D IT GO?" SARAH popped into Jamie's kitchen to check in after Max's morning appointment at the hospital.

"Max is fine. Doctor says he will probably only vaguely remember this whole ordeal when he's older," Jamie replied as she prepared sandwiches for lunch. "We saw Boo, as Max has named her. I tried to thank her but didn't do a very good job I'm afraid. I was all choked up." Jamie's eyes held back tears just thinking about what might have happened if not for Boo's quick action. "Have you eaten?" Jamie asked her sister.

"I had something, thanks. I'm catching up on some paperwork down at the office. First time I've felt like working since this happened. Talked to Mom and Dad again today and finally convinced them Max is fine and they do not have to rush home. They said from the stories in the news it sounds like Max is near death. I can't believe those fucking so-called reporters," Sarah fumed.

"Bryan told me one story had the police and social workers crawling all over this place, and I was about to lose custody or some such nonsense. He just wanted to warn me in case someone said something."

"Speaking of police," Sarah took the opportunity to change the subject, "Chief wants to stop by. Said she had a little more information to share. I told her to come by about three. Hope that's okay."

"That's fine."

After lunch and a nap with Max in a shaded hammock on the back patio, Jamie heard Chief call from the gate. Jamie buzzed her friend through and met her at the front door.

"Is this official business?" Jamie hugged her old friend.

"Mostly, but I also wanted to check in on Max, and you. How is my little buddy?"

"He's fine, we received a good report from the doctor." Jamie nodded her appreciation of Chief's concern.

"We found the man who picked up our hero's backpack. He barely remembered it. He was high on something. Said he took the cash from a wallet and a camera. Swears he threw everything else away and did not pocket a phone, and doesn't remember seeing any name or anything else. He was focused on the cash, about a hundred dollars. Said the camera was a superzoom, but nothing fancy. He sold the camera to someone for $50. He couldn't tell us who and didn't care. He just wanted the money. We checked the dumpsters around where he says he threw backpack away, but it was long gone to the landfill. We notified the people out there, but it's a long shot that anyone will ever find it. We'll see if we can find the camera, maybe it has some pictures on it, but that's also a long shot."

"That's not much to go on. Do you think we should post a reward for information? I'll put up the money if you think it would help."

"At this point, I think that would bring trouble, people calling us with things just to see if they can get the money. Let's hold off. I talked to our hero briefly. She has no idea how she ended up here. No accent I could detect. Maybe that makes it less likely she's from the south or New England where they tend to have heavy accents. That doesn't narrow it down much. The doctor said memory loss would not make her lose an accent."

"I'll listen more carefully next time I talk to her." Over the course of her career, Jamie had spent many weeks with accent coaches preparing for roles. "Maybe I'll pick up on something. After all, I have imitated almost every regional accent at some point or another." Jamie was already looking for excuses to see Boo.

"We obtained some surveillance video from a couple of stores and from the city building. We found her walking in front of the city building about five minutes before the incident. Came from the north headed south. We have a better picture of her now and sent our people out to stores and restaurants to see if anyone recognizes her. Nothing yet. We are also checking for abandoned cars or if someone is supposed to be in a hotel room but hasn't been. In other words, she had to come from somewhere and be here for some reason. Failing all that, sooner or later we're bound to find a missing person report on her. She doesn't look like a stray."

Jamie nodded, taking it all in. "I saw her today at the hospital. I don't remember seeing her before Saturday. I think she has the kind of strong face I would remember if we had interacted. And she's tall for a woman, so I think that would have made an impression. I'm really sure I would have remembered her voice if we had talked." Jamie relived the pleasant sensation the low timbre of Boo's voice caused in her body.

"That makes me feel a little better she's not a stalker or something." Chief wanted to say, *unless we have a new one*, but instead added, "It's my job to be suspicious. And to serve and protect."

Jamie smiled fondly at Chief. Their long history included a few intense, scary moments when Jamie was stalked by someone with delusions of being in love with her, or more to the point—one of her characters. Chief spent a couple of sleepless nights guarding the house until the creep was caught. The guy fit the description of *psychopath* to a T.

"Will you please let me know if you find out anything or if there is anything I can do?" Jamie offered.

"Will do. If you need anything, call or text me." Chief made her way out to her car to return to the station and continue monitoring the progress of this mystery to be solved.

• • • •

JAMIE MADE AN EXCUSE to go to town the next day and stop by the hospital. Walking past the atrium cafe, Max suddenly yelled *Boo* and took off toward a woman dressed in gray sweatpants and a dark blue T-shirt, courtesy of the local fire department. Chief was seated across from Boo. Both were standing by the time Jamie caught up. Max was already in Boo's arms for a hug.

"Makes you feel a little second best, doesn't it?" Chief put a protective arm around Jamie.

"Not a bit." Jamie leaned into Chief, gazing admiringly at Boo holding Max.

As Max reached over to hug Chief, he kept his legs wrapped around Boo.

Raising her eyebrows and nodding toward Max, Boo silently mouthed the question, *Ice cream?* Jamie nodded yes.

"Hey, Max, want some ice cream? They brought chocolate today."

Max looked at his mother, who nodded her okay.

"Yes! Can we bring Mom and Chief some, too?"

Boo looked at the two, who both politely declined. Max and Boo headed toward the staff break room while Jamie walked down the hallway beside Chief.

"Did I interrupt something?" Jamie asked.

"No, we were just talking. I brought in a map of the US to see if anyplace prompted a memory. Nothing yet. Seems she has no clue why she is here in Crestwood or how she arrived here. We have started trying to match up missing person reports in other states and took her fingerprints to run through the databases."

"Max seems really attached to her. What do you think?"

"Not sure," Chief pondered for a moment, "I admit, she is charming as all get out, in a good way. Thoughtful, polite, impeccable manners. In fact, the nurses are calling her Boo Charming now. I can see it."

As they reached Boo's room, Chief excused herself, promising to keep in touch with any new developments. Jamie involuntarily smiled at the sight of Boo and Max talking about the map of the US as they bonded.

"Chief said the map didn't spark anything yet. How are you feeling?" Jamie pulled in a chair to join them.

"The doctor said I am more likely to have older memories at first, from years ago. I remember being in a forest, near a mountain. I was looking for something but don't remember what. I can't bring up any names or where or when it was. Hopefully things will keep coming back to me. I feel…disconnected. I realize everyone else has a family and home to go to, and here I am, with no home, and no one I can remember."

"If there's anything I can do to help, please tell me. I can't even imagine what you're going through, but I don't want you to feel alone." Jamie did the best she could in the moment, but felt inadequate in her effort to comfort the woman who had saved her son.

Boo looked at Jamie with a genuine expression that wanted nothing.

The intensity of the warm feeling spreading through her body startled Jamie. She suddenly realized, outside of her close friends and family, this was the most real she had felt with anyone in a long time.

Chapter Four

JAMIE AND MAX VISITED the hospital every day for the rest of the week. Boo physically looked better each day. The doctors had performed an MRI right after the incident and another a few days later. There was evidence of a minor brain bruise but no changes that looked troubling. This was good news for Boo's prospects for full recovery. Boo still suffered headaches and was dizzy and light-headed at times. Otherwise, she ate well, regained her motor skills, and concentrated for longer periods of time.

Boo interacted with Max effortlessly, occasionally looking up to politely ask Jamie something about her life.

"Are you originally from Crestwood?"

"Yes, I was born and raised here. I went away for a while, to New York City, but this has always been my home."

"What was in New York City?" Boo said the name of the city carefully, turning it over in her mind as if a memory connected to it might appear.

"College." The question was innocent, but out of habit Jamie censored her answer. "I guess I needed to experience the big city in order to appreciate coming back here. And when I adopted Max I wanted him to be here with family and people I trust." Jamie stopped herself short, wondering if she was saying too much, but Boo didn't seem to notice the habit of mistrust pervading her answer.

"Do you have other kids?"

"No, just Max. I've been thinking about adopting another child. I would like for him to have a sibling. I love having a sister. I sometimes feel like I would be depriving him, growing up without a sibling. Plus I love being a parent. I would love to have another child in our family." Jamie had not shared her feelings with anyone outside her immediate family and closest friends, but the story tumbled out of her mouth in Boo's presence.

"I guess I don't know if I have kids. I don't know who is out there looking for me." Boo wistfully smiled at Max, before asking Jamie, "Are you married?"

"No, I'm not. Max and work keep me busy. And I'm surrounded by family."

"Sorry if that was too personal. I seem to be a little preoccupied with other people's families while I wait for mine to show up."

Jamie reached out, squeezing Boo's hand with hers. She could feel the worn callouses on the upper palms of Boo's large hand. Although it was an innocent gesture of compassion, when Jamie removed her hand from Boo's, she could still feel the warmth of their touch.

"I'm sure you have a family and it's just a matter of time before we find them for you." Jamie paused. "I'm sorry. That sounded so cliché. But I really do believe we will find them. Until then, Max and I are your family." Jamie's words were not a mere offer, but a declaration.

"Chief came by earlier today and told me they found a waitress at a diner on the highway north of town who remembers me. She said I came in and ordered breakfast. Paid with cash. I said something about meeting someone in front of the library and asked directions. Then I took off walking. They assume someone dropped me off from the highway. They are hoping the person I was supposed to meet will come looking for me. Still no clue why I'm in Crestwood. I guess it's not exactly on the way to anywhere."

True, Crestwood was not a destination town. The rural, small town feel was exactly what Jamie loved about her hometown. Almost everyone there had known her since she was a child, so Jamie was not subjected to gawking or autograph requests. Even the paparazzi left her alone since there was no one else in the area who interested them. A *zero-zone* in their words, meaning there was no money to be made from hanging out in Crestwood. Except for the twelve hours after Max's near-death when a few of them showed up hoping for a tragic storyline. Like Sarah said, they were like vultures looking for fresh kill—sometimes too literally.

"I hope someone turns up looking for you soon. How much longer will they keep you here in the hospital?"

"I'm not sure. They don't seem to know what to do with me." Boo face betrayed her distraught feelings at the thought of being cast out. "One of the nurses offered to take me home with her, which is really kind, but I don't want to be a burden on anyone. On the other hand, I don't have any money or ID or even clothes besides what they've been nice enough to bring me. I have no clue how I'm going to pay the hospital bills. I guess if I'm lucky, I have health insurance." Boo sighed her resignation.

Jamie felt a tinge of jealousy at the thought someone else might take Boo home. She wanted to wink and tell Boo she rocked the donated clothes, but stifled the urge. Instead, she tried to put Boo's mind at ease about the hospital bills.

"I did some checking. The hospital will not be charging you for the treatment. They'll write it off."

Jamie did not explain she had this knowledge because she already had a discussion with the hospital administrator. All charges would be written off on the community services ledger Jamie's family underwrote in order to provide care for local people who otherwise could not afford it. All incidentals would be billed directly to Jamie, although the ice cream seemed to be a donation by the nursing staff.

Jamie's eyes turned to her son.

"Max, I have an idea. Why don't we ask Boo to come home with us when she's finished here at the hospital?"

"YES!" Max threw himself into Boo's arms. He talked to her with all of the sincerity of a four-year-old, "You can come home with us. We have a big dog. Her name is Fred. You can meet Uncle Bryan, and Aunt Sarah, and Marco, and Gee. They have horses. And Grandma and Grandpa. They are in Florida right now, but they'll be home soon. Right, Mom?"

"I have to ask my doctors," Boo looked at Max, although she was speaking to Jamie, "And your mom needs to think this through. It's a big responsibility."

"I would not have offered if I didn't think it was a good idea," Jamie replied. "Selfishly, I want to know you are okay. We have a big house. We'll follow the doctor's orders and bring you back here for your appointments. And don't worry, if there is news, Chief will find you."

Boo contemplated the offer on the table. "Thank you. We'll talk to the doctors."

* * * *

"YOU WHAT?" SARAH'S tone indicated that she wasn't really asking a question.

"I asked her to come home with me. It just seems right. She doesn't recognize me. She's not trying to hurt us. She's doesn't have anyone. It's just temporary. I'm sure they will find out who she is or she'll remember. Then she'll be gone." The last thought left Jamie inexplicably sad.

"How do you know she doesn't want to hurt you? How do you know this isn't just an elaborate hoax and she's playing everyone? She may...I don't trust her." Sarah was three years older than Jamie and had always played the role of protective big sister. When Max arrived, Sarah became even more protective.

"Sarah, yes, there have been a few crazies. That's part of the business. But this isn't a movie of the week. This is someone who just needs someone else to care, for now. Stop trying to protect me from things I don't need to be protected from."

"Well, that's the problem. We don't always realize we need protecting until it's too late. And it's not just you. You have to think about Max, too." Sarah had to look out for her sister, especially when Jamie threw all caution to the wind. Sarah planned to call the Chief as soon as she got home. Maybe Chief could talk some sense into Jamie.

"Okay, now that that is settled...I bring Boo home Monday morning." As she said it, the word *home* resonated with Jamie in a new way.

· · · ·

JAMIE SPENT THE WEEKEND preparing the guest room and researching memory loss, concussions, and brain injury care. When she arrived at the hospital Monday morning, the nurse took nearly thirty minutes giving instructions and handing her a book size collection of printouts.

"I hope you understand what you're doing, Jamie." The doctor expressed her concern as they walked toward Boo's room, "We still don't know who she is or where she's from."

"Did my sister call you?" Jamie rolled her eyes. "Don't worry, I got this. I once played the target of an amnesiac assassin. It was a great movie. I think we called it *The Forgettable Killer*." Jamie and the doctor both laughed. "Yeah, not one of my finer roles."

"Okay, you know this is not a movie. Just follow the instructions, and if you notice any changes in behavior or how she feels, bring her back immediately."

Jamie nodded her understanding of the doctor's orders as they entered Boo's room.

"Wow, you clean up nicely!" Jamie surveyed Boo's lean muscled body, which had been hiding under the ill-fitting donated clothes. It took considerable effort for Jamie to stop herself from staring at Boo lest her eyes betray a less-than-noble interest in her soon-to-be houseguest.

Boo was dressed in khaki pants and a bright red T-shirt emblazoned with the words *I do all my own stunts*. Jamie and the doctor were amused by the choice of Jamie's assistant, Shon, who had picked out the new outfit and delivered the clothes to the hospital the day before.

"Remind me to thank..."—Boo closed her eyes to concentrate—"Shon, for the clothes. Like, really, remind me. I'll forget between here and there." Boo tried to remember things for longer periods of time, but did not always succeed.

"Shon's at the house with Max. You will meet them soon," Jamie said.

"Let's sign you out." The doctor held forth a piece of paper and a pen pointing to a blank box with an X.

Boo looked at the box for a moment, then took the pen and signed *Boo Charming*.

"I overheard the nurses say that's my new name, although I'm not sure if it's legal."

Jamie signed the next line, indicating Boo was released into her care.

"You're all mine now." Jamie winked at Boo before feeling self-conscious. "Mine and Max's," she added, grabbing the bag with the rest of Boo's donated clothes and meager belongings.

Boo followed Jamie down a back stairway to a service entrance where the delivery trucks parked. The truck that had struck her ankle was parked at the loading dock, but Boo seemed to have no recognition of it.

"I park back here because it's more convenient for getting in and out of the hospital." Jamie told the half-truth in response to an unasked question. The full answer was that parking at the loading dock was more convenient for avoiding any paparazzi who might be lurking about. She also failed to mention the wing of the hospital they walked through was paid for in part by the Jordan Family Foundation. Given that and her fame, hospital security had no problem letting her drive in and out the guarded entrance without question.

It occurred to Jamie that this was the first time she and Boo would be alone together. Of course she met and spent time with a lot of strangers, and a lot of strange people. But those people were almost always in the context of her work. She had been on a few dates over the past couple of years, but only when friends she trusted set her up with someone. Each date had been, to put it mildly, a disaster. So, Jamie resigned herself to being Max's mother and concentrating on family and work. She sometimes missed the romance of having a girlfriend.

Boo interrupted Jamie's thoughts. "I have to warn you the doctor said I might have some motion sickness. I'd hate to thank you for your kindness by throwing up in your car."

"I have a four-year-old, a niece, a teenage nephew, and a very large dog. If you think this car has not seen a little spit-up, vomit, bloody elbows, mud, and been peed on several times, well, you would be sorely mistaken," Jamie laughed. "But thank you for your concern and I will try to take it slow so hopefully you won't feel the need to throw up. Now, are you ready to go home, or do we need stop for something?"

"I think I'm ready." Boo climbed in the SUV. More than she wanted to admit, she liked that Jamie had used the word *home*. "I can't think of anything. I have a few clothes I can wear. Shon guessed my size so these clothes fit great. I wonder if I have always been this stylish?"

Jamie had described Boo's physique to Shon as best she could. She was used to thinking in terms of costumes and listening to designers talk. Shon did a little shopping and came up with a few outfits they thought a good fit for Boo's size and apparent personality. There were more outfits waiting for Boo in Jamie's guest room.

"Shon does a lot of my shopping. They have great taste. They will take you to town to do your own shopping once you feel up to it. The doctor still wants you to avoid a lot of excess stimulation." Jamie emphasized the last two words, wondering exactly what activities the doctor was referring to.

Boo was a puzzled by why Jamie had someone else do her clothes shopping, but it seemed too personal to ask about.

"I have something for you." Jamie reached into the SUV's center console and handed Boo a cell phone.

"Thanks." Boo looked blankly at the phone as though she had no idea what to do with it. "That's really very generous of you. I'll pay you for it when I figure out..."

Catching Boo's hesitance, Jamie wanted to make her more comfortable with the gift.

"We programmed it with my number, and Shon, Sarah, Bryan, Chief, your doctors. I guess we could put in a couple of delivery places in case you don't like my cooking." Jamie had never given her personal phone number to anyone outside of family and close friends. She had other phone numbers for business and work-related friends.

"I've been eating a lot of hospital food lately. I think your cooking will be just fine. And hopefully I can help. Maybe that's a good thing about losing my memory, maybe I forgot I'm a lousy cook and I can become a great chef now. I'm looking for my next career move since I forgot my last one." Boo's sense of humor about her situation was positive and served as a cover for the pain and uncertainty of her condition.

The rest of the fifteen minute ride home was mostly quiet, with a few comments about the scenery. Boo finally closed her eyes to combat the queasiness brought on by the motion.

As they pulled off the highway into the gated driveway, Jamie looked over at an already weary Boo. "Ready for the next chapter in your life?"

Chapter Five

A QUARTER OF A MILE along the paved driveway, a small house appeared on the left, nearly obscured in the summer months from the main road by the woods around it. Jamie identified it as her office and the office for the family business. Another quarter mile brought an unassuming, sprawling one story limestone ranch house into view. The house was in a clearing in the woods, with a gravel lane off to the right. Jamie pulled into the attached two car garage.

The house was just the kind of ordinary house Jamie wanted to be her home. Not huge but enough space for her to raise children and welcome family and close friends. Walking into the kitchen from the garage, Boo was prepared for Max's lunging welcome but not Fred's greeting. Fred was short for Frederica, a one hundred and twenty pound soft black Newfoundland, who greeted Boo with a nose to the crotch and a wagging tail.

"Whoa, what a welcoming committee," Boo held Max in one arm as she reached down to scratch the dog's head with her free hand. "This must be Fred!"

"Well, it sure ain't Shon. When I greet people like that, they tend to get a wee bit testy," Shon said as they walked into the room. Shon was a slender six feet tall. Their ten inch coils of amber hair accentuated their glowing sepia brown skin and beautiful long lashes framing warm brown eyes. "I'm Shon," Shon extended a hand in greeting. "I see the clothes fit. And we'll do something about that, soon," Shon waved a hand at Boo's half bandaged, partially shaved head. A nurse had attempted to even out the bad emergency room buzz and wash away the blood after the stitches were put in, but Boo's hair was still a mess.

"Thank you. I have some donated clothes, but these fit much better. You look about the same size as me. Are you my long-lost sibling?" Boo and Shon giggled as though they were indeed from the same flock.

"Okay you two, if you can somehow manage to cut short your reunion," Jamie joined in the banter. "Please take Boo to her room and I will make some lunch. Shon, please stay. And remember, Shon, low stimulus." Jamie narrowed her eyes into a stern look of warning against her assistant's sometimes overly enthusiastic approach to life.

Shon cast their eyes downward as if they intended to obey the order but the outlook for compliance was doubtful.

Max and Fred led the way to Boo's room on the backside of the house. This wing had a large TV room with a sectional sofa, a guest room, and a bathroom. In the guest room was a king sized bed and large French doors leading to the patio and pool. The view behind the house was rolling hills covered with woods.

Shon unpacked Boo's few belongings into a dresser in the corner along with the other outfits they had ordered. Max took Boo on an abbreviated tour of the rest of the house, ending up in Max's room where he wanted Boo to read to him. Jamie found them there ten minutes later with Boo quietly reading one of Max's favorite stories to him. Boo's Spanish was good, although her American accent was evident.

"A dónde va la perrita?" Boo asked Max, pointing to the picture of the dog in the book.

"No sé. Va a comprar helado." Max smiled at Boo.

"No, dogs should not eat ice cream." Boo chuckled at her young friend's sense of humor. "It's bad for them. But maybe...tal vez está buscando a sus amigos para jugar."

"Sí, she's looking for her friends. So they can eat ice cream!"

Boo continued reading from the book as Max commented on the pictures in a mixture of Spanish and English. Jamie watched for a moment from the doorway before interrupting them.

"Time for lunch. Max, would you please put your book away and show Boo where she can wash her hands?" Jamie requested before she returned to the kitchen.

"I saw a car on the monitor this morning driving past the gate slowly, four times," Shon reported. "Gray four-door sedan. Looks like an airport rental. I would guess paparazzi just look-seeing."

Jamie's eyes conveyed her dismay but any further exchange was interrupted by Max running into the room with Boo close behind.

Boo lifted Max into his booster seat, then looked around the kitchen, taking in the large island and big dining table where people obviously gathered for family meals. Jamie and Shon brought lunch to the table and everyone was seated.

"There's a pool out back if you want to use it," Jamie offered.

"Thanks...I'm not sure if I know how to swim, plus I'm not supposed to get my head wet." Boo, uncertain how to handle such offers until she could remember her abilities, changed the subject. "Shon, where are you from?"

"Brooklyn originally. But I gave up all that excitement to come work with the wonderful Jamie Jordan!" Shon gave a flourish with their hand before seeing Jamie flinch. In the friendly confines of the kitchen, they had forgotten to be guarded.

"How old are you?" Boo asked. The nurses estimated Boo's age as forty in the medical chart, but short of carbon-dating some part of her body, it was not clear how they made their educated guess.

"I'm twenty-six. I have a BA in Theater Administration and minored in Business. I'm hoping to open my own talent agency someday."

"I'm four." Max held up three fingers, then corrected himself by adding the fourth.

"He just turned four last month. And I'm thirty-nine," Jamie added. "Boo, have you remembered any other places you may have been? The doctor said you might see things when you left the hospital that would spark a memory."

"No clear memories. It was nice to see big trees and rolling hills. When we drove by the lake, I remembered being in a canoe on a lake, somewhere." Boo had visibly relaxed since leaving the hospital and town, seeming more at ease.

"We can borrow a friend's boat sometime, take a picnic, go out on the lake, if you think that might help." Jamie noted to herself that she was picturing an idyllic day on the water and Boo was definitely a part of the picture.

For the remainder of lunchtime, Shon entertained everyone with exaggerated stories of growing up in New York City, meeting Jamie, and moving to Crestwood. Max asked if Shon would take him and Boo to visit the Statue of Liberty. It was clear that, in a child's eyes, everyone at the table was already all one big, happy family.

After cleaning up the remnants of lunch, Shon headed back to the office as Boo, Jamie, and Max went to their respective rooms for naptime.

• • • •

VOICES WOKE BOO FROM a sound sleep. Walking toward the sound, Boo paused near the kitchen door. She did not recognize the voice of the woman speaking to Jamie.

"Are you sure about this? Do you really know what you're doing? You can't just bring strangers into the house. What if she isn't *perfectly lovely*?" Sarah drawled out the last phrase.

"Everything is fine. She is not a stranger. We just don't happen to have a lot of information about her yet. And, yes, she is perfectly delightful company and Max and Shon and Fred all agree with me," Jamie sighed her exasperation with her sister.

It was true. Max was bonded with Boo. Shon and Boo acted like old friends. And Fred had taken a liking to Boo after smelling her crotch, which seemed like a perfectly reasonable test to Jamie.

"Fine. I'll sleep over tonight just to make sure."

"Fine, but if you sleep over you can't snore, and you have to take the two a.m. feeding." Jamie's smug look was tempered by the memory of Sarah staying with her for the first two weeks after Jamie adopted Max as an infant. Sarah had joyfully risen in the middle of the night to feed Max, giving Jamie some extra rest.

Before the conversation could continue, Boo flushed the toilet in the bathroom to signal she was awake. She walked into the kitchen, rubbing her sleepy eyes.

"How long have I been asleep? Oh, hi. I'm...Boo."

"I'm Sarah, Jamie's sister."

"It's great to finally meet you. I have heard a lot about Aunt Sarah from Max. He clearly adores you. And I'm really looking forward to meeting the rest of your family."

"It's good to see you up and about," Sarah returned Boo's smile with a twinge of guilt about her indictment. "You look much better in person than the picture Chief showed me." Even totally heterosexual Sarah couldn't help but notice the allure of the tall, muscled figure in front of her and she began to question her sister's motives for inviting Boo home.

"How can I be helpful? I don't want to just hang out all day eating your food. Is there something I can do?" Boo offered.

"How about you take the first day off," Jamie said it more like an order than a request. "Get acclimated to being out of the hospital and settle in. Sarah, do you think Marco and Gee could come and take Boo for a short walk? Show her the lane between our houses?"

"Sure, I'll call Marco. Lord knows he's glued to his phone." As Sarah headed out the door, she called over her shoulder, "It was nice to meet you, Boo. I'll be back later."

"Are you sure it's okay I'm here?" Boo asked after Sarah left the house. "I don't want to cause any tension between you and Sarah."

Jamie sighed, realizing Boo had overhead the conversation between sisters.

"Sarah is intense, and intensely protective of me. It's really not about you." Jamie shook her head before adding, "Max and I, and Fred and Shon, are all very happy to have you here. It just takes a while for Sarah to warm up. Please make yourself at home."

Jamie checked the message on her chirping cell phone. *Marco and Gee are on their way.* Jamie went to Max's room where he was quietly reading to Fred.

"Please put your shoes on. It's time for a family walk."

Marco and his twelve-year-old sister, Gee, arrived shortly. The group walked the gravel lane to Sarah and Bryan's house, then to the stable behind. They were greeted by two calm, old, chestnut-colored horses, swatting flies with their tails. Perfect riding horses for children.

Boo walked slowly, absorbing the shade of the trees into her skin. A memory formed of hiking on a trail through a forest, carrying a heavy backpack, with other people whose faces she could almost see but not picture clearly. She was brought back from her vague, distant memory by a large, yellow butterfly fluttering in front of her face.

"Look, a papilio glaucus—eastern tiger swallowtail." Boo's memories for some things was clearly intact.

* * * *

SHON LEFT THE OFFICE for the day, headed back to their apartment in town. Sarah and Bryan eventually joined the rest of the family for dinner at Jamie's house. Boo attempted to help cook dinner but apparently had little muscle memory of this particular activity. Everyone made small talk, trying to not overwhelm Boo like family gatherings sometimes do to newcomers. Marco apologized to Boo for causing *this mess.*

"Max is safe, all is forgiven." Boo patted Marco on the back, endearing her to Bryan, but Sarah retained the leery look on her face.

Boo excused herself for an early bedtime while Jamie settled Max in bed and read him a story. Jamie retired to her bedroom, where Sarah was already in bed reading. Jamie shook her head at her sister's determination to be her protector, wanted or not.

"The doctor wants me to check in on Boo a couple of times during the night, just to make sure everything is okay. Said I didn't have to wake her, just make sure she's breathing and looks comfortable. So, I'll take the two o'clock check if you'll do the five on your way out the door in the morning?"

"Fine," Sarah replied before turning out her light and promptly beginning to snore.

To wake herself without setting an alarm, Jamie drank two glasses of water just before bed. It was one-thirty when she woke up, needing to pee. Jamie made a trip to the bathroom before crossing the living area to the guest room door.

She looked in quietly, not wanting to disturb Boo. The bed was empty. Jamie panicked until she noticed the door to the patio ajar. She had not turned on the house alarm since this was Boo's first night. She did not want Boo to accidently set it off and scare everyone to death.

Jamie walked through the open door to find Boo asleep on a lounge chair on the patio near the pool. In the nearly full moonlight Jamie could make out Boo's face, softened by sleep. A very peaceful sleep she noted.

The fresh air was almost intoxicating. Jamie feared Boo would wake up and be confused by her unfamiliar surroundings. With Sarah in the house in case Max woke up, Jamie grabbed a blanket from Boo's bed and settled into a nearby chaise.

"My first night with Boo," Jamie whispered to herself as she drifted back to sleep.

Chapter Six

CLOSE TO SUMMER SOLSTICE, the sun rose early. A cardinal singing just before dawn's first light woke Jamie. She looked over at Boo, who was still sleeping. Rising silently, she slipped into the guest room to return the blanket to Boo's unused bed. There was no sign of Sarah yet.

Boo had seen Jamie asleep in the chaise during the night. But Jamie's disappearance in the morning light made Boo think that she might be embarrassed by her action. When Jamie reappeared on the patio, Boo stretched and acted as though Jamie had just appeared outside for the first time that morning.

"Good morning. I hope it's okay I slept out here. I was having a hard time getting to sleep. I thought some fresh air might help."

Jamie sat on the end of the chaise facing Boo. "It's fine. I hope you slept well. My sister snores, so there wasn't much sleeping going on in my room." Jamie was aware of how convincing she was when telling half-truths. "Would you like some breakfast?"

"Only if I can help you make it." Boo hopped up from her make-shift bed to follow Jamie into the kitchen.

"How are you feeling this morning?" Jamie asked, assessing Boo's morning demeanor.

"Okay. Not sleeping in a hospital is much better. I had a dream I was in a boat. Probably because we talked about that yesterday. I was calling out to someone who seemed to always be just out of reach. Zoe. Do you think it's someone in my family?"

"Maybe. We'll text Chief. The more clues we have to work with, the better."

· · · ·

IN THE OTHER WING OF the house, Sarah opened her eyes enough to look at the clock.

"Five-thirty, damn!" Sarah rolled over. Jamie was missing. She ran her hand over the pillow. Cold.

Sarah rushed toward the kitchen, certain that Jamie was in danger. She stopped short at the domestic scene of Boo chopping green and red peppers while Jamie whisked eggs into an omelet pan and watched over bagels in the toaster oven. Sarah took a deep breath and exhaled loudly, calming the panic she had manufactured in her barely awake state.

"I slept late. Sorry. I need to go home. Is everything okay?" Sarah gratefully accepted the cup of tea Jamie slid across the kitchen counter toward her.

"Yes, everything's fine. The birds are singing. It's a beautiful morning."

Sarah raised a quizzical eyebrow at the cheer in Jamie's voice and made a mental note to ask about it later.

"I'm headed into town this morning to Mom and Dad's to pick up a few things and check their mail. Do you want anything?" Sarah sipped the tea while the smell of breakfast made her hungry.

"What time are you going? Boo has a nine o'clock appointment at the hospital. Would you mind taking her and I'll pick her up later?" Jamie made a schedule in her mind. "Boo, is that okay?"

"Absolutely. I hate to be a bother, although I doubt they'll give me a driver's license until I have a name. Maybe I could buy a bike and ride into town. It didn't seem far."

"No!" Jamie and Sarah simultaneously pronounced the prohibition.

"It's really not safe to ride on the highway around here. Too many blind spots on the road." Jamie turned to her sister, "Sarah, what time are you heading in?"

"I'll pick her up at eight-thirty," Sarah called over her shoulder as she left for breakfast with her family.

There were still a couple of hours to enjoy the morning. During breakfast, Jamie and Boo talked quietly. Neither acknowledged that Jamie had joined Boo on the patio the night before.

"I'm sorry, I never asked—what kind of work do you do?" Boo's face furrowed as she sorted through her memory of the previous day's conversations. "Bryan said at dinner last night that he's an accountant in town. We drove past your office yesterday. You said you have a family business."

Jamie needed to make a decision about what to tell Boo and when. The house was devoid of clues about her work. She kept her home separate for herself and for Max. At his age, Max did not understand her job. He occasionally traveled to location with her, but was too young to understand or even remember much. To him it was simply a long play date with other kids of the people working on the set. Jamie carefully tucked away the awards and honors in her office. There was also a pile of scripts waiting to be read for a decision about her next project.

"I'm taking a bit of break from work right now. An extended vacation if you will. Shon will be in the office if you need them. Just give them a call and they will come up to the house. I have someone who helps me take care of Max when I travel, but I like time alone with Max when I have a break." Jamie expertly evaded the real topic Boo had asked about.

"Oh, sorry, am I interrupting your family time? I can find someplace else to stay."

"No, that's not what I meant. I mean I like to give Max my attention and re-charge my own batteries. When I'm here I don't like to think about or talk about work much. Max will only be a child for a short time. It will fly by and I don't want to miss it."

"Sarah and Bryan and their kids are great. Your parents live in town but are away? Will they be back soon?"

"Yes, they'll be back next week. My mother is a semi-retired lawyer, meaning she is as busy as ever, mostly doing pro-bono work for the women's shelter and a few community groups. My father is a retired minister. He created a community garden with the women and children at the shelter. The kids there love him. He's like a grandfather figure. They are in Florida right now with my aunt, Dad's sister, who isn't doing very well."

Max walked into the kitchen, rubbing his eyes with his un-splinted hand. He went directly to his mother for a morning snuggle, then to Boo, who lifted him onto her lap. Max had adjusted to his temporary one-handed state and started to eat the bagel and omelet in front of him with his uninjured hand, not realizing it was Boo's breakfast plate.

A warm rush filled Jamie's body as she looked at the scene across the table. Max was the love of her life. Boo was starting to affect her in ways she did not expect.

· · · ·

SARAH ARRIVED PROMPTLY at eight-thirty to pick up Boo. They barely made it to the highway before Sarah spoke in a serious tone.

"Look, you saved Max and we all appreciate that. A lot. But Jamie can be...impulsive." Sarah wanted to say *my sister can be stupid* but censored herself, adding instead, "I will not let anyone hurt my sister. Not on my watch."

Although Sarah did not make an outright accusation aimed at Boo, given the ferocity of her tone, she did not have to.

Boo thought about Sarah's point of view. A stranger in her sister and nephew's house would definitely seem like a possible threat. Or, maybe, Sarah saw Jamie sleeping outside on the patio next to her and was suspicious of Boo.

"I really don't want to cause any problems for Jamie or you. If you think it's best, I'll ask the nurse again if I can stay with her for a while, until I can make better arrangements."

"That might be easier on all of us. I don't want to see Max get attached to you and hurt when you leave. Eventually you'll remember your name and go home. You have another life somewhere." Sarah was clearly intent on saving her sister.

The remainder of the drive to the hospital was filled by tense silence.

* * * *

"YOU FUCKIN' WHAT? YOU told her to find someplace else?" Jamie could not remember ever being this angry with her sister. "You take your sorry ass over to the hospital right now and apologize. No! You fucking stay away from her. And me, too, for now. This is unbelievable. I will fix it myself. Don't you fucking..." Jamie hung up on her sister, immediately dialing Boo's cell phone, hoping it was turned on.

"Hello?"

"Boo,"—Jamie calmed herself, lowering her voice—"I just spoke to Sarah. She told me what she said to you. She was way out of line. It is not true. I want you here," Jamie told the truth more clearly than she intended. "Max wants you here."

"Thank you, Jamie. I don't know what to say. I don't want to come between you and Sarah. She's right. Maybe it's unfair to Max if he becomes attached to me and then I remember everything and leave."

"I will pick you up as planned." Jamie took a deep breath and exhaled. "Please? Let's talk before you make other plans. My sister is over-protective and there are reasons. I'll explain if you give me a chance. Please?" Jamie was on the verge of outright pleading.

"Okay. I don't want to be a source of problems for anyone."

"Great. Just text or call me when you are done with your appointments." Jamie ended the call before Boo could change her mind.

• • • •

SEEING BOO WALK OUT of the physical therapy clinic, it was all Jamie could do to resist clinching the woman into a relieved embrace. She let Max deliver his customary leap into Boo's arms instead. Max had insisted on coming with her. Although Jamie hoped she would not need the emotional advantage in order to convince Boo to come home with them, she knew that resisting Max's enthusiasm would be futile.

Fortunately, it seemed as if Boo had forgotten the earlier conversation with Sarah. Boo climbed in the SUV without discussion. They stopped for take-out and pre-lunch ice cream on the way out of town.

"What did the doctor and PT have to say?" Jamie inquired while licking the ice cream cone in one hand and driving with the other.

"No real change. They are pleased with my progress." Boo licked a drip from the side of her cone. "I said something to the doctor about Marco reminding me of my nephew. When the doctor asked me his name, I said Michael. Didn't think about it. Just said it. Doctor said that would happen. I would just say things without thinking—an automatic response. I guess that's a big clue, I have a nephew, so I must have a sibling, so someone must be looking for me. I hope." Boo was notably cheerier talking about the prospect of finding her family.

Jamie barely suppressed a grin watching Boo intently licking the ice cream cone, then reminded herself silently to get a grip on her growing feelings of attraction.

• • • •

AFTER LUNCH, BOO READ Max a story and tucked him in for a nap. When she returned to the kitchen, she was pleased to find Jamie still at the table. The intense warmth of Boo's eyes caused Jamie to look away.

"Is everything okay?" Boo asked, concerned she had offended her host.

"How about naptime, then we'll talk?" Jamie had been caught reflecting on when and how to tell Boo the truth, or at least more of it. She was not ready, yet.

Boo nodded her head and retreated to the guest room. Jamie made her way outside to lay down on the chaise on the patio where she slept the night before. Drifting off to sleep, she tried to gauge her feelings and what to tell Boo about her life.

Chapter Seven

MAX WOKE UP FROM HIS nap and went to the kitchen to find his mother.

"Can I go in the pool?"

"Yes, put on your swim shorts and a sun shirt, please. We'll re-tape your fingers and put a dry splint on after you get out." Jamie sometimes allowed Max to skinny-dip, but the sun was intense today and his young skin would sunburn quickly. Plus, there was someone else in the house now.

Max hurried to his room to change clothes. He ran back through the kitchen in a flash, heading out the door with Jamie a few steps behind.

All Boo heard through the open door to the patio was a loud splash followed by a child's screams. Five long strides later she dove into the pool before she was even fully awake. Seeing Max flailing in the middle of the pool, she swam underneath him, lifting him out of the water. A couple of quick kicks propelled their bodies to the side of the pool, where she placed Max safely on the ledge.

"Are you okay?" Boo gasped for breath.

"Again!" Max giggled as he jumped over her head into the pool.

Jamie caught Boo's arm before she could leave the side of the pool to save him again.

"It's okay, he can swim. He's had lessons, and he has his floats on."

Only then did Boo see Max's inflatable armbands. The flailing and screaming was playful, not an indication of distress. Boo relaxed her muscles, dropping her head against the side of the pool, embarrassed by her actions. She struggled slightly to lift her fully clothed body out of the water. Sitting on the edge of the pool, dripping, Boo's shoulders sagged.

"It's okay," Jamie reassured Boo, "you thought he was in trouble. You just wanted to help." Jamie sat down next to Boo, dangling her legs in the cool pool water. "On the bright side, you can swim."

"I was dreaming. I was running through the woods trying to catch someone. But they were always just out of reach." Boo's eyes filled with tears.

Jamie moved closer, putting an arm around Boo's shoulders. Jamie felt the water dripping from Boo's head.

"Oh no, we weren't supposed to let your bandage get wet. Your cut is still healing. We better take you to the doctor. We keep the pool clean, but any number of nasty things could be living in there."

"Damn...sorry. I guess I haven't forgotten how to cuss. It does sting a bit. Sorry. I'm sure it will be fine until tomorrow. I don't want you to have to drive back to town. Maybe Shon can take me when they go home and I'll find a place to stay tonight."

"Alright...no." Jamie pretended to be in control of the situation. "This is how it's going down. I will ask Shon to come up from the office and watch Max. Then I'm taking you to the hospital for a dry bandage and make sure everything's okay. Then we will come home, together, and all watch a nice quiet movie after dinner. Deal?"

"Maybe I should put on some dry clothes first." Boo lifted herself from the poolside and retreated to her room.

As soon as Shon arrived and Boo emerged from a quick rinse in the shower and dressed, Jamie drove Boo to the hospital. She parked by the service entrance and found one of the nurses from Boo's previous stay. Even though she tried not to take advantage of her privilege too often, Jamie appreciated the special efforts staff made for her.

"Good to see you again, Boo Charming," the nurse winked. "When a nurse says that to you, it's probably not a good thing. Let's see what we have here."

The nurse slowly peeled off the wet bandage, revealing an irritated, bright red wound. She gently cleaned the cut, treated it with an antibiotic, and put on a fresh bandage. Boo was released with strict instructions not to dive head first into the pool, or anything else for that matter, for at least another week.

On the drive home, Jamie reached for Boo's hand, giving it a reassuring squeeze.

"I talked to Chief while you were in with the nurse. She said nothing turned up on the search of your fingerprints. Apparently some departments are not reliable about submitting everything or lose records, but she's pretty confident you have been a very good person and never been incarcerated or arrested. She also said you are most likely not a police officer or other first responder. She's looking into a couple of other databases."

"So I'm not a serial killer after all and just conveniently forgot that little detail. That's good news."

Jamie grinned at the unwitting inside joke. She was chickening out of the talk she needed to have with Boo.

"The doctor said personality does not change with this kind of memory loss. I am betting we're all safe. Would you do me a favor and watch Max for a couple of hours while I go down to the office to work with Shon?"

"Absolutely," Boo responded without hesitation.

* * * *

JAMIE SPENT THE REMAINDER of the afternoon in the office with Shon. First, the two sorted through recent invitations for personal appearances, some of which Jamie would politely decline herself and some of which Shon would respond to on her behalf. Then, there were a couple of endorsement offers to consider. Jamie disliked giving endorsements, but the contracts were lucrative and kept her name in the public eye even when she was not actively making films.

"What do you think about the car offer?" Jamie was on the phone with her agent for their weekly meeting. While her agent was savvy, in Jamie's opinion he was sometimes too aggressive in pushing her brand image.

"I think it's a good one. Not risky. You would have to drive the car for at least a year, to make it look legit. I'll ask for the specifics and timetable. What about the software startup?"

Start-up and tech deals were difficult to judge. It was impossible to foresee which startup would tank and leave the endorser looking like a fool, and which would take off and make the endorser look like a genius. Either way, the companies had tons of money to throw around.

"Let me think about it. I'll have Shon do some research. They're my tech genius. I'm too old to keep up with all this new stuff." Jamie winked at Shon, who sat on the other side of the desk taking notes.

"Let me know which script you want a read for. We don't want to pass up too many good ones or they'll think you've retired and start looking elsewhere."

Jamie's agent was pushing for her to commit to a new production soon. Although Jamie would have to admit that her agent was right and she needed to choose from the scripts on her desk, she was enjoying her time off. She liked setting her own schedule, and spending time with Max. Plus, right now, she did not want to leave until Boo had recovered and found her family.

As if reading her mind, Jamie's agent inquired, "Is there anything I need to be aware of? The story about Max faded within 24 hours. Thankfully Ray-Ray got himself arrested after a bar fight—all on video. Amaya broke up with her boyfriend and released a song about it two days later. The press moved on. But, there has been some gossip."

"Yes, the person who saved Max is staying with me. We don't know her name or where she's from. The police are working on it. The paparazzi seem to have lost interest for now. We haven't seen anyone around." Jamie let her tone convey her annoyance at the intrusion into what she considered her personal life.

"Are you sure this is safe? This could be a stalker or a gold digger or some-one...publicity is good, but we don't want any additional bad publicity."

"Look, it's all fine. She's none of that. Do people even still say *gold digger*? I will let you know if I need something." The implication that Max almost being killed was bad publicity irked Jamie. She finished the call quickly and turned to Shon. "I swear, I've had enough of people wanting to save me from Boo."

Shon said nothing but the look on their face let Jamie know that they agreed wholeheartedly with her on this issue.

When Jamie returned home, she was greeted by the smell of marinara sauce simmering on the stove and bread warming in the oven. Boo and Max looked up from their dinner preparations with self-satisfied smiles.

"Max said your favorite meal is spaghetti?" Boo looked hopeful.

"I think what Max means is his favorite meal is spaghetti!" Jamie nuzzled her son's ear and kissed him on the cheek, causing him to giggle. Then, before thinking, she kissed Boo's cheek too. "I'm famished. Is it dinnertime?"

Max carefully carried a large bowl of salad across the kitchen to the table. Boo delivered the pan of spaghetti while Jamie grabbed the bread out of the oven.

"Looks like a feast. Are you sure you're not a chef?" Jamie helped Max fill his plate.

"We cheated. I found a cookbook on the shelf. I tried to use the computer but it has a password lock. I guess I could have used my phone. I didn't think about it."

Jamie felt guilty for keeping Boo isolated from the digital world. "I'll write down my password in case you want to use the computer. And we'll hook your phone into the wi-fi."

"Great, I'll check my email later," Boo stopped. "Oh—do you think I have email?"

"I'm pretty sure it's not possible to avoid email these days. We can create a new account for you, if you want? Maybe your email name could be Boo dot Charming or something like that."

Dinner conversation was light, followed by watching an animated film about a lost fish, one of Max's favorites. Max sat between his mother and Boo on the large sectional sofa in the TV room, alternately snuggling up to one and then the other. At one point tears fell from Boo's eyes as she empathized with the sad, lost fish.

"Which fish are you, Mom?" Max asked innocently at the end of the film.

After a moment of panic, Jamie regained her composure.

"I guess I would be the Momma fish. Now, it's time for you to get ready for bed."

Jamie followed Max to his room. After reading a bedtime story and tucking him in, she returned to find Boo surfing channels on the TV. Fortunately Boo was watching a softball game on one of the sports channels. The odds of seeing something Jamie appeared in on this channel were extremely low.

"Max requested that you to come say goodnight, if you feel like it. I told him that you've had a long day."

"Of course. I'd love to. I'll be right back."

Jamie turned off the TV and grabbed the book sitting the end table, flipping the pages mindlessly until Boo returned.

"I think I'll head to bed too. Thanks for everything today. I'm sorry I caused you to make two trips to town. I'll do my best to stay out of trouble tomorrow."

Boo's shy look, her dimple accentuating her lips, caused Jamie's heart to melt a little more.

Chapter Eight

BOO, JAMIE, AND MAX settled into a weekday routine. Jamie or Shon would drive Boo into town for her appointments, followed by lunch, a nap, an afternoon walk, and pool time for Max. Shon helped Boo order clothes online to expand her wardrobe. Jamie maintained veto power over the more outrageous of Shon's T-shirt choices for Boo. Chief stopped by a few times to update Boo and ask questions to help narrow the search field.

Boo remembered more each day. While she recognized some names and places as familiar, none were connected yet in ways to provide definitive information about her identity. Walking along the lane and through the woods, Boo provided ongoing educational commentary, sharing the names of plants, birds, and butterflies.

"Rose-breasted grosbeak. It must be nesting time around here."

"Common milkweed. It's where the Monarchs lay their eggs and what the caterpillars eat."

"Red-winged blackbird. One of the most common birds in North America."

"Look, cypripediuma—a lady's slipper. Oh, and myosotis scorpioides, also known as forget-me-not. Someone must have planted these here."

"We should hang a white sheet tonight, with a light behind it, and see how many moths we can attract. They should be out this time of year." Boo's excitement was contagious and Max was an enthusiastic apprentice.

"You seem to have a lot of knowledge about birds and plants." Jamie noticed how easily this part of Boo's memory was returning. "Do you think it's related to your job?"

"I'm not sure, maybe. It feels like I've always known this stuff. The doctor said established memories would come back first. Maybe it's just a hobby I've had since I was young."

Jamie's phone pinged three times. She absent mindedly picked it up to check the text from Shon. "María Garcia called and wants to talk to me. Okay."

"María Garcia...that name..." Boo's face conveyed the startling effect of sudden recognition.

"Really?" Jamie shifted uncomfortably, trying to contain her unease.

"She's...my spouse. Do you know her?" Boo's admission shocked both her and Jamie.

"You're married?" Jamie focused in on Boo's marital status, forgetting to explain that the María Garcia in the text had been married to the same man for over 25 years. María Garcia was also a famous director, who won several awards for a film Jamie starred in.

"I think we're married. Is she calling about me?" Boo looked lost as she strained to sort out the memories.

Jamie attempted to manage the confusion of feelings overtaking her, a mixture of happiness that Boo had a family who would be looking for her and loss at the thought of Boo leaving. She reached for Boo's hand.

"No, she's calling about my work. I'm sorry, Boo. The María Garcia who is contacting me is married, to a man, and has been for a long time. But this is a big clue. You have a spouse who must be looking for you."

Jamie typed *María Garcia* into the search bar of her phone's browser.

"Only one-hundred sixty-four million results. Well, that narrows it down. Can you remember where you were married, or when, or any other details?"

"I don't remember where or when. I remember her family. They are somewhere in Texas. We celebrated holidays with them. Her brother is Miguel. And a niece and nephew...María and Antonio. I can't remember his wife's name."

Jamie added the new information and pressed the search button again. "Okay, that narrows it down to only three thousand four hundred and seventy nine records of a Miguel Garcia, related to a María Garcia, living in Texas. There are lots of pictures of María Garcia's online. Let's pull them up on the computer screen and you can look at them while I call Chief and give her the new information."

Boo spent the next hour looking at pictures online until her eyes glazed over.

"I don't see anyone I recognize. Maybe we're divorced. We did fight about my work and my being away from home a lot." Boo conveniently left out the part about remembering dating other women. She wondered if she had been caught cheating on her spouse.

"I've heard that before." Jamie cringed, remembering the complaints of her former partner about her work schedule. She changed the subject. "I'm headed to Fairfield after lunch to pick up Mom and Dad at the airport. Would you like to come with me?" Jamie wanted to spend as much time as possible with Boo, who might remember her name at any moment and leave her life forever.

"Will there be enough room in the car?"

"Sarah is taking Max with her to Marco's soccer practice, so it's just me. I'd love to have your company and maybe the drive will shake loose more memories. Fairfield is about an hour drive northeast of Crestwood."

"Sounds great. I'm looking forward to meeting your parents."

Between Max and Shon and the rest of the family coming and going, Boo and Jamie rarely spent a lot of time alone together. This seemed like a good opportunity to simply enjoy each other's company.

As Jamie's comfort around Boo increased, she spoke more off-handedly about working in the film industry. On the drive to the airport, Jamie reminisced about locations she visited without being specific about the particular reason why she was there. Sometimes Boo would recognize a town and share a story about being in the same spot. Jamie began to wonder if they had met before, or at least been in the same place at the same time. Usually if she wondered this about someone she was talking with, she became less trustful. In Boo's case, it made her feel more connected somehow.

"Do you think people can start over? Build a new life, new memories? Without being captive to their past?" Boo asked what for anyone else would be an existential question, but for her was entirely practical.

"I doubt anyone our age can have a truly clean slate." Jamie kept her eyes on the road as she drove. "I don't believe in destiny or anything like that. I think we learn and grow from our experiences. Everything we experience is an opportunity."

"I'm sure things have happened to me to make me who I am. But since I can't remember a lot of those things, I wonder, who am I? Is this really me?" Boo silently wondered if she had ever felt about someone else the way she felt about Jamie. Given the likelihood she was married, the question seemed inappropriate.

"I don't think losing some of your memories changes your essence. You are kind and obviously smart and clever. You are always thoughtful with Max. You've been remarkably patient and positive about this whole ordeal. I think I would have been much more frustrated and angry."

48   *EL Bossert*

"Really? I can't picture you angry. Well, except maybe with your sister, but I think that's more family dynamics than anything."

There had been a slow thaw of Jamie's feelings towards her sister over the past week. Their love bound them to each other regardless of their current disagreements. Big sister being over protective of little sister was one of their ongoing tensions.

"You've only seen me in one place, at home with Max and my family. I can be different when I'm at work."

"Have you ever been in love?"

"Yes," Jamie consciously decided to tell the truth, "I've been in love a couple of times. Or at least what, at the time, I would have called being in love. I think the definition changes as I age."

"Do you mind if I ask what that was like? I remember being married but I don't remember being in love. I must have been in love or at least thought I was if I married someone, right?" Boo, absorbed in sorting out her feelings, pondered her capacity to fall in love in the present moment.

"The first time I fell in love was right after college. I was living in New York and out on location for the first time. It was a very overwhelming experience and there were all these intense emotions. Amelie was beautiful, glamorous, older than me, and I fell head-over-heals. She was kind but for her the relationship had an expiration date—the end of the job. We stretched it out a bit, then she was off to her next job, and person, and I was left wondering what I did wrong." Jamie had not discussed her first relationship with anyone but her closest friends. She left out the part about the seduction of shooting twenty takes of a love scene with Amelie. "It feels kind of good to remember it now. I learned a lot. It made me wiser."

"You said you've been in love a couple of times." Boo repeated the statement without asking for more information.

"I have. The second time—the last time—was with Jenn. We were together for seven years. She's an artist. We met in New York, moved in together, then she moved back here with me. But there was nothing here for her. It was too quiet, and I'd be gone for weeks, or months even. It just didn't work out." Even years later, remembering Jenn leaving was sad for Jamie.

"When did you decide to adopt Max? Was that something you and...Jenn wanted to do?"

"Jenn and I talked about having kids, but always put it off. I guess after Jenn left, I realized I shouldn't keep putting my life on hold for the next job. I always wanted kids, so I started the process. Took two years before Max came along. It was the happiest day of my life to bring my baby home. It felt like a new beginning. I'll admit, what I've been putting off since then is any new romantic relationship."

Boo understood the statement as a clear message that Jamie was not available for a relationship. Not that it mattered since, in all likelihood, Boo herself was married.

As they drove into the airport, Boo mused out loud, "I think this is my chance for a new beginning. I hope I don't blow it."

Using the VIP entrance to the airport was a perk of Jamie's fame. Being unseen was good for airport security because it kept people from running toward her or crowding in one place, often to the inconvenience of other passengers and families. It was good for Jamie because she could easily find her parents, grab their luggage, and be on their way before anyone discovered they were there.

"What are your parent's names?" Boo had only met them via video link. "All I hear is Mom and Dad, or Grandma and Grandpa."

"Mom's name is Alessandra, but her friends call her Lessa. Dad's name is Philip."

Jamie's parents appeared through the lounge door, rushing across the room to hug Jamie. They recognized Boo standing demurely a couple of feet away and pulled her into the family embrace.

"You are much taller in person. Oh my." Lessa's eyes twinkled as she realized Boo was the reason for Jamie's good spirits over the past week.

"Thank you for coming with Jamie to pick us up. I was hoping we would meet you soon." It did not take long for Philip to come to the same conclusion as Lessa.

"It's a pleasure to meet you both, finally, in person." Boo felt relieved that Jamie's parents did not seem to be as suspicious of her as Sarah was.

"Let's get you two home." Jamie picked up one of the bags and directed them to the car. "Do we need to stop for anything?"

"No, we're fine. We had lunch during our layover in Charlotte," Philip replied.

Lessa sat in the front passenger seat next to Jamie, while Philip climbed in the back seat with Boo. The hour drive to Crestwood flew by as Lessa and Philip provided an update on Jamie's aunt's condition and recounted all of the news and gossip from her father's side of the family.

Sarah brought Max and the rest of the family to Lessa and Philip's for a family homecoming dinner. The grandchildren were excited to see their grandparents, all talking over each other as they shared recent events. Max had already forgotten the harrowing experience leading to the splint on his hand. In fact, he was already having a hard time remembering his life before Boo arrived.

Chapter Nine

JAMIE TUCKED MAX IN after Boo had read him a story. She turned off the light in Max's room and returned to the kitchen to finish cleaning. She saw Boo standing in the dim moonlight on the patio by the pool and contemplated for a moment the striking, noble woman. Jamie felt guilty for not telling Boo the whole truth. She took a deep breath and walked out into the pleasantly warm summer evening.

"Thank you for joining us for family time today." Jamie stood by Boo, looking out on the dark hills speckled with thousands of flashing fireflies. Jamie could feel the heat of Boo's body next to her even on a warm evening.

"Thank you for sharing it all with me. I feel very fortunate to be included. Your parents are wonderful. They made me feel very welcome." Boo's happy expression had the slightest hint of sadness. "I hope I have a family like that, out there somewhere."

"Boo, I need to tell you something." Jamie came close to blurting out everything she had not said for the past week, but her resolve failed at the last instant. "I am flying to New York City tomorrow evening for a work meeting on Monday. I'll be back late Monday night. Max is staying with his grandparents and they said you are welcome to stay with them also. Or you can stay here. Shon is not going with me. They will be here during the day and can take you anywhere you need to go. Bryan and Sarah and the kids will be around too. I don't want to leave you stranded out here since you haven't been cleared to drive yet."

"Would you mind if I stay here? Or I could get a room in town if you think it would be better. Well, I mean I can borrow more money from you to get a room. I don't want to impose on your parents. Or Shon. You've all been extremely kind and generous. I don't know how I'll ever repay you for what you have already done for me."

"Repay me? Are you kidding?" Jamie attempted to act at least half as incredulous as she felt. "You are welcome to stay here as long as you need or want to stay. I want you here." Jamie had never invited anyone to stay in her home when she was not there. Her habit of distrust and strong need for privacy kept this her sanctuary. But, for now, this was Boo's only home. Jamie took one of

Boo's hands in hers and leaned her head toward Boo, resting it on Boo's shoulder.

The sheer tenderness of the moment both reassured and caught them off-guard with its intensity. Their inhale and exhale of breath co-mingled in the sweet evening air. Before Jamie could lean in for a kiss, Boo abruptly pulled away, closing her eyes and sighing deeply.

"I should probably head off to bed now. I hope you sleep well." Boo retreated inside to the guest room before she no longer had the will to leave Jamie's presence.

Jamie stood for several minutes, rooted to the spot on the patio where she had almost kissed Boo, contemplating her increasing feelings of attraction. It was impossible to say what she did or did not know about Boo. But her own feelings were becoming clearer with each day they spent together.

The following morning, Jamie and Boo walked carefully around the other in the kitchen. Neither wanted to give away that the night had been a dance of tossing and turning fitfully, punctuated by steamy dreams, leading to more restlessness. Fortunately Max woke up early and joined them, immediately dissolving the tension as they engaged in their morning routine.

Jamie spent the day preparing to leave and packing Max's overnight bag. Boo took Fred for a long walk and then sat on the patio by the pool. Through the open window, Boo heard Jamie in the kitchen on the phone.

"Yes, Boo is staying here while I'm gone...No, she doesn't need to go somewhere else...Yes, I'm sure about this...Why don't you fuckin' get over it, Sarah. I'll tell her when I'm ready."

The last line of the one-sided conversation begged the question Boo had wanted to ask the past couple of days. Jamie clearly did not tell her everything. Then again, why should she? Their relationship was borne out of what? Necessity? Convenience? Pity? Part of Boo wanted to know answers to lots of questions. But for now she was taking great comfort in being in Jamie's home, and in Jamie's presence. And, Max also. At this point, hesitation at disturbing this routine won out over her curiosity.

Jamie interrupted Boo's thoughts, appearing on the patio and plopping into the chaise lounge.

"Let's not even pretend. I know you heard me on the phone with Sarah. I try to not be mad at her, but she can be so infuriating." Jamie sighed and continued, "There was a stalker, several years ago. A real whack job. He got as close as this patio before Chief caught him. Sarah was totally freaked out. He's in prison now, mostly for some other crimes he committed. But Sarah just became overbearing about protecting me after that, and even more now with Max here."

Boo's face betrayed her alarm and concern as she listened.

"Anytime anyone new gets close to me," Jamie paused to compose her story, "she's just convinced they are out to hurt me or take advantage of me. I thought when Shon first arrived Sarah was never going to let them out of her sight. She practically stalked Shon until I finally confronted her and told her if she didn't stop I would move. It took her a while, but now she trusts Shon. I think the same will be true with you. She just can't let herself trust you, yet. She's not used to me having someone here that she doesn't know."

"Will this whack job come back? Why would anyone want to hurt you?" Boo's confusion mixed with a protective urge.

"We know where he is right now. Chief will tell me if and when he is released from prison. Apparently he assaulted a prison guard, adding some time to his sentence. I try not to think about it. You can't understand crazy. If you try it just drives you crazy and let's someone else control your life."

Boo was a captivated audience, but opted to let Jamie offer the information rather than asking.

"Is there anything I can do so Sarah doesn't feel like I'm a threat? I could stay somewhere else?"

"For the thousandth time, no. You will stay here. Neither of us will be happy if we give in to Sarah's paranoia. I really believe she will come around. Now, do you have everything you need before I leave?"

"Yes. There's food. I have the phone. Shon will be here tomorrow morning. I don't have any appointments. I thought while you are gone I'll build Max a treehouse." Boo's smile was sly but earnest.

"If you can find the scrap lumber and a sturdy tree, have at." Jamie imagined Boo's strong arms lifting loads of lumber and hammering them into form.

Jamie felt better having told Boo more while still not totally coming out about her work. She realized there was risk in leaving Boo alone in her house. Boo could innocently surf channels on TV and come across one of Jamie's movies, hear Jamie's voice on a commercial, or a picture might appear on the internet while Boo was online. This risk seemed minimal, however, since Boo had shown little interest in watching TV outside of a couple of sports and nature channels, and she spent little time online except to check out information related to new memories.

If Boo did find out, then they would have a long talk about Jamie's reasons for not telling her before. It would be a test of their relationship, whatever that meant. Or the end of any future relationship they might have. Jamie would take the chance.

By mid-afternoon, Jamie and Max had left the house and it was quiet except for Fred's constant company. Fred kept a close eye on Boo, as if she were personally in charge of protecting Boo as part of the family. Boo felt confident that, if something happened to her, Fred would run all the way to town to retrieve Chief or Shon. At least that was the comforting fantasy.

Boo, able to concentrate for longer periods of time now, spent part of the evening reading the book from the end table she had seen Jamie reading. She was curious about what Jamie was interested in. At dusk she walked outside to the patio to breathe in the warm, dry summer air.

Boo closed her eyes and pictured Jamie swimming with unselfconscious grace in the pool. She remembered the way Jamie moved through the pool with power and ease. She imagined Jamie's toned body, gliding through the water with each stroke. Boo felt an urge to run her hands over Jamie's body, to feel her curves instead of just staring at them from afar.

Fred's bark brought Boo back to the present. She shook her head to push the thoughts of Jamie's body out of her mind. She was a short-term guest in Jamie's life, although she wondered if there could be more and if her feelings toward Jamie were reciprocated. Until she discovered her identity, and found out if she was still married, Boo was stuck. Keeping her attraction to Jamie under control was imperative.

Boo dozed on the patio for a few minutes before returning to the house, locking the doors, and crawling into her bed.

• • • •

IN NEW YORK CITY ON a warm early June evening, Jamie met her best friend for dinner. She enjoyed the hustle of the city as a change of pace. It reminded her that life moved faster other places, and also why she left the city for someplace quieter.

"So, tell me more about this new person in your life?" Gabriela did not hold back when talking to Jamie. That was why they became friends in college and had remained close over the ensuing years.

Gabriela had heard the basic story—Boo saved Max, lost her memory in the process, and had no idea who Jamie was. Gabriela listened between the lines to the emotions in Jamie's voice as she talked about Boo. It was hard to keep secrets from an old friend, even when Jamie wasn't ready to admit things to herself.

"She's...a wonderful mystery," Jamie settled back in her chair, "a gift I don't yet know if I get to unwrap and keep. I almost kissed her the other night—"

"Almost? What stopped you?" Gabriela was surprised and intrigued.

"She pulled away and went off to bed. Alone. Probably for the best...I just feel...so drawn to her. She treats me like...a real person, a friend, a confidant. It's not a relationship tied to anything else. I loved Jenn, but this is different. It's a clean slate, for now. Someday I'll have to tell her or she'll find out about my work."

"Sweetie, it's not like you're a porn star. Not that there's anything wrong with that." Gabriela laughed out loud at Jamie's lack of perspective. "You act. It's your job. We all work. Maybe you need some grounding. And maybe, just maybe, you need to trust that someone loves you for you."

"Who said anything about love?"

"You don't have to, querida, I can hear it when you talk about this Boo Charming."

The rest of the evening was spent as long-time best friends do, reminiscing, catching up, and sharing their feelings unguarded. This was the grounding Jamie needed right now.

Chapter Ten

SARAH SLAMMED OPEN the front door and burst into Jamie's house just after midnight.

Startled awake from a sound sleep, Boo heard Sarah yelling as she raged through the house.

"Where is she? What have you done with her?"

Fred barked as the ceiling light in the guest bedroom switched on, temporarily blinding Boo.

"Where is she?" Sarah repeated. "I know you know where she is."

Boo gathered her thoughts as quickly as she could. "Jamie is in New York. I thought you knew."

"Not Jamie, you fuckin' creep. Gee! Where's Gee? And her friends?"

"Gee?" Boo's confusion slowed her thought process. "I have no clue—isn't she at home, with you?"

"Jamie's gone, you're here alone. I told Jamie you were trouble. Chief's on her way. Tell me where you took Gee! Now! Before I fuckin' kill you."

Sarah moved toward Boo, but Fred intervened, positioning her large body in front of Sarah just enough to slow her down. Boo scrambled out of the far side of the bed.

"What are you talking about? I haven't seen Gee. I was asleep. I wouldn't hurt—"

Boo's protest of innocence was interrupted by Chief running through the bedroom door. Chief grabbed the panicked, possibly homicidal mother from behind.

"Whoa, stop it, Sarah. Boo doesn't know where Gee is." Chief trusted her instincts, and Jamie's, believing Boo would harm no one. "I talked to Bryan on my way here. I have a couple of officers right behind me. We'll organize a search and find Gee and her friends." Chief loosened her grip on Sarah only slightly.

The adrenaline coursing through Boo's body brought clarity to her mind—Gee was missing and Sarah thought she had kidnapped the child. The accusation left Boo sick to her stomach as she literally shook the sleep from her head and focused.

"I haven't seen Gee, or anyone else. I have no idea where she is. I went to sleep a couple of hours ago. I haven't—"

"It's okay, Boo, we'll find her. Sarah, we need to go to your house now and get organized. Boo, you stay here. No use in you getting lost in the dark." Chief half guided, half dragged Sarah out of the house and into the car.

"What the heck, Sarah? Boo has nothing to do with this. We need to find Gee and her friends and this is not helping." Chief barely contained her anger at Sarah while trying to focus on the task at hand. Chief hoped this would be a simple trek through the woods where, as often was the case for missing children, they would find three lost, hungry, cold children who thought it would be fun to go out in the dark of night. That was the best possible ending for this story.

The other officers were waiting for Chief at Sarah and Bryan's house. Bryan relayed the basic facts to everyone. Gee had two friends staying overnight for a slumber party in the basement. When Sarah went to check on them, the three girls were not there. Sarah yelled for Bryan and they searched the house, then the barn. Gee's cellphone rang in the basement when they tried to call her, and there was no answer on the other girls' phones and no reply to texts. They called Chief as they continued the search inside and outside of the house.

When Bryan shook Marco from sleep, the young man confessed Gee and her friends had talked about taking a midnight swim. He did not believe they were serious and ignored them.

Bryan had waited for Chief at home while Sarah drove the lane toward Jamie's house, searching.

The sheriff's dispatching officer was enlisted to contact the other girls' parents. One of the officers started a trace on the last cell phone signals for Gee's friends' phones.

The most likely place for Gee and her friends to swim was the lake. There was a two mile trail from the property to the nearby lakeshore. Gee had hiked the trail many times for summer swims with her family. She could find her way there by staying on the trail. With flashlights, it would be a relatively easy, if ill-advised trek.

Grabbing the truck keys, Sarah and Marco took off for the lake with one of the officers. They would search the area and walk the trail from the lakeshore back toward the house. Bryan and Chief would begin at the house and walk toward the lake. Another officer would wait at the house for the parents of the other girls and in case the girls appeared back at home.

• • • •

BOO FELT NAUSEOUS AFTER Sarah's accusation that she could harm a child. Although it was understandable that Sarah was panicked, this was extreme. Boo resolved that in the morning she would figure out how to move somewhere else until she could piece her life back together. She wondered if she should call Jamie but decided this was for the family to decide.

To clear her mind and shake off the horrible feeling in the pit of her stomach, Boo pulled on a pair of jeans and boots and stepped outside. Fred, sensing something was wrong, followed her closely, holding her nose in the air as if searching.

A sound came from the west. Far away and muffled by the wind, Boo dismissed it as a bird or animal. Then she heard it again. The sound originated from the hills over which the sun had set.

Fred lumbered off toward the path leading into the woods.

"Fred, come back," Boo called to the disappearing dog. "I don't need for this night to get any worse."

Fred turned her head to look at Boo but ignored the plea.

"Darn it." Boo grabbed a small flashlight from inside the kitchen door and stepped off the patio in the direction she had last seen Fred.

The night was lit by only half a moon high in the sky. The fireflies added twinkle but were little help in piercing the darkness.

"Fred, come back here, please."

Fred appeared just within sight, then lumbered off again.

"This is not the time for a walk, Fred." Boo realized she was attempting to reason with a dog. On the other hand, right now, the dog made far more sense than the humans. Boo continued to follow.

"Fred, where are we going? Are you trying to tell me something?" Boo saw car lights driving toward the front gate. She heard two voices on the path toward the highway, yelling the girls' names. Boo did not want to distract anyone from their important search. Plus, she had been ordered by Chief to stay put.

An order she was now disobeying. Although, she reasoned in her own defense, she was just following the dog.

Fred kept up the back and forth, appearing and disappearing, leading Boo to the west. It was a path they had walked several times in the daylight, but the heavy darkness rendered it unfamiliar. The small flashlight barely penetrated the blackness of the deep woods to illuminate the dirt track worn by years of people and animals walking the same line.

Seeing only a few inches in front of her feet, Boo walked into several low limbs. Crickets kept a steady chirp around her. Occasionally animals scurrying through the woods created a noisy ruckus. The beady double eyes of snakes glowed from the side of the trail. Most were garden-variety non-venomous snakes, but there were also copperheads in these woods who were nocturnal during the warm summer months. Boo tried not to think too much about how or why she knew this fact.

Fred and the trail were leading in the direction of the sounds Boo heard earlier.

"I hope you know where we're going, or we are in big trouble." At this point, Boo wasn't clear if she was talking to Fred or herself. She put her trust in Fred, figuring if they found someone or something she could call Chief. Otherwise, no harm done. Unless a snake bit her or she fell into a hole. Then she would need to rescue herself to avoid delaying the other search mission.

Boo and Fred traveled a little under a mile in fifteen minutes. They came to the area of a large pool in the creek that flowed between the hills. Boo had been by it several times on her daily walks in the woods. There was a steep drop-off, about thirty feet on the near side of the creek, and a small rocky beach on the other bank. Boo had been told that the kids were not allowed to swim here because of snakes and other unseen creatures that might be lurking in the waters.

As Boo approached the cliff, she heard two children crying.

"Gee? Is that you?" Boo called into the pitch black.

"We're over here. Hurry," young, frantic voices called back.

Fred led the way towards the voices while Boo reached for her phone to call Chief. When there was no answer, Boo left a hurried voicemail explaining where she was. She followed Fred and the voices to two girls huddled on a flat rock at the top of the cliff. Boo did not recognize either of them.

"Where's Gee? Is she okay?"

"She's down there. She fell off." The girls pointed over the edge of the cliff.

Boo carefully peered over the edge, pointing her flashlight into the darkness.

"Gee?"

"Boo?" Gee's voice sounded weak. "Boo, help me."

Boo could barely see the young girl, wedged into a two feet wide crevice between the side of the cliff Boo was standing on and a rock jutting out below. Using the dim flashlight, Boo surveyed the small outcrop. The drop was about seven feet to a four feet wide by ten feet long ledge.

"Do you have flashlights?" Boo shone her light on the two crying girls, clinging to each other.

"Our phones died."

"Use my phone. Stand here and shine the light right there." Boo directed them to the spot she wanted lit. "Don't move. If I can't get back up, you need to call for help. Okay?"

The girls nodded.

The faint cucumber odor wafting in the air was the scent of a copperhead. Boo spotted snake eyes to one side of the ledge. A copperhead bite would be painful but not deadly. The other side of the ledge looked clear.

Boo heard someone in the distance calling her name. Fred barked a loud response. The phone rang but the girls held it in position.

"Help me, please," came the plea from below.

Boo immediately jumped to the lower ledge. A seven foot drop was a lot farther than she remembered. Then again, she did not remember a lot of things very clearly these days. Her momentum almost carried her off the lower ledge toward the creek pool twenty feet further below, but she landed in a wide stance and caught her balance. A rush of adrenaline kept her from noticing the sharp pain in her right ankle, the same one that was hit by the truck when she saved Max.

The snake made a lightening quick strike towards Boo, then recoiled. It was too far away to make contact and slithered off the far side of the ledge into the darkness.

Boo took the flashlight out of her pocket to illuminate Gee. Most of the girl's small body was wedged in a crevice.

"Gee, can you move?"

"I'm afraid if I move I'll fall. My leg hurts."

"Okay, I'll put my arms under yours to lift you up." Boo had been in good shape a couple of weeks ago, and the physical therapist was working to maintain her muscle strength, but even in top form this would be a tough position to lift Gee from.

Feeling dizzy and lightheaded from the jarring landing of the jump, Boo sat down to prevent herself from falling over. She braced her legs on the side of the cliff she had jumped from, one on each side of Gee.

"Alright, when I say, you try to move your arms and grab me." Boo put her hands as far as she could under Gee's arms. "Okay, now, grab my shoulders."

Gee froze in fear.

"Gee, you have to trust me. Just grab my shoulders and climb up."

Boo was vaguely aware of a voice calling from the near distance above her and the girls screaming back, *hurry,* while Fred barked encouragement.

"Come on, Gee."

Gee finally took hold of Boo's arms, working her hands up to Boo's shoulders. Boo lifted enough for Gee to kick herself free as Boo pulled her onto the ledge. Boo scrambled to her knees, shining the flashlight to assess Gee's condition.

"Are you hurt?"

"My ankle. It hurts," Gee cried.

There were scratches all over Gee's legs and arms, but nothing was bleeding profusely. In the flashlight's beam, Gee's ankle looked bruised and swollen.

A large spotlight appeared from above. Chief peered down at the two dusty figures stranded on the ledge below.

"Are you two okay?"

"I think Gee might have a broken ankle. We need to get her to the hospital."

"Bryan is right behind me. He's bringing a rope and a horse to carry her out. Can you lift her up to me?"

"I think I can." Boo forced herself to her feet.

Gee hesitated, her entire body shaking.

"We can do this." Boo spoke the words calmly, trying to reassure Gee, "I'll brace myself against the side of the rock and lift you up. Even if you fall, you will just fall right back down on me. You can't fall down there again. I promise. Ready?"

Gee nodded, allowing Boo to lift her up until Chief, crouched on her knees on the ledge above, could safely reach for the child. Chief grabbed Gee's arms, lifting her the rest of the way up. With the three girls now safe, Chief turned back to Boo.

"It's okay. I'll hang out here for a few minutes. Or, I might go for a swim. How dangerous could that be?" Boo hoped she sounded more nonchalant than she felt. She had a throbbing headache and the ground beneath her was doing a slow, wavy dance.

"Hang tight. We'll throw you a rope and have you up in a minute."

Bryan and the officer from the house arrived on the two horses. Sarah and Marco were on their way back to the house to join the other parents.

A rope was tied off on a tree and lowered to Boo, who expertly tied in a few knots and climbed the cliff face. Chief and Bryan fashioned a splint for Gee's ankle from sections of a tree branch and the rope. Bryan put Gee on the horse in front of him while the other two girls were led out on the second horse.

Boo limped heavily and slowly back to the house, sometimes leaning on Chief to steady herself. Fred led the way, refusing to leave Boo behind.

"Boo, what were you thinking? You could have gotten lost, or hurt even worse? I thought I told you to stay put." Chief shook her head, imagining she would have done the same thing in these circumstances.

"It's all Fred's fault," Boo replied somewhat truthfully, although both she and Chief knew good and well she would have been out looking for the lost children with or without Fred's lead.

Chapter Eleven

WALKING AROUND THE side of the house, Boo could see Gee in the back of the ambulance with Sarah at her side. The other two girls were being driven to the hospital by their parents to be checked out although they had no apparent injuries. As paramedics removed the temporary splint on Gee's ankle and started an IV line, the ambulance driver closed the doors for transport. When the ambulance left for the hospital, Bryan and Marco and a parade of cars followed close behind.

"How about a ride?" Chief gently led Boo to her Sheriff's car, making the order sound like a polite request. "Keep this up and we'll hire you as our one person search-and-rescue squad."

"I need to take Fred home and lock the house. I let Jamie down," Boo slurred the words. "I left the house open and need to check and make sure no one is in there."

"I'll make sure Bryan and Sarah's place is locked. We'll drop Fred off and check Jamie's house. Then I will drive you to the hospital." Chief continued, more to herself than Boo, "If something happens to you, Jamie will never forgive me."

Exhausted and disoriented, Boo barely mumbled *okay* as she mostly fell into the front seat of Chief's car. She laid her head against the cool dashboard to ease the throbbing pain.

Chief, recognizing the distress in Boo's demeanor, put Fred in the back seat and jumped in the driver's side of the car. "We'll just go straight to the hospital. I'll call for backup." Chief guided the car along the dark driveway toward the highway. She used her private phone to call for assistance to prevent the request from being broadcast on monitored frequencies. Officers were immediately dispatched to both houses.

Keeping her eyes on the road, Chief called Shon to send them to Jamie's house. Sirens on, Chief sped down the road toward the hospital, silently praying to the goddesses no deer jumped into the road tonight. It could be deadly for all of them.

• • • •

SOUND ASLEEP IN GABRIELA'S guest room, Jamie was startled awake by her phone ringing. When she saw her mother's cell phone number on her screen, she panicked, fearing the worst.

"Mom, what's wrong? Is Max okay?"

"Max is fine. It's okay, honey, I just wanted to tell you that Gee hurt her ankle and they are headed to the hospital. I didn't want you to hear it on the news in the morning."

"What happened?" Jamie's breath was fast and shallow.

"It's a long story. I also need to tell you that Boo has a headache and Chief is bringing her to the hospital."

"What? Is she okay? What is going on there?"

"We'll tell you in the morning. Everyone will be fine. I'm headed to the hospital now and I'll stay with Boo. Don't worry, we'll update you."

"Right...no. I'll be home as soon as I can arrange a flight."

"Honey, we all know you're working—"

"Mom, don't even try, I'm already packing. I'll be there as soon as I can." Jamie hit the button to end the call before her mother could protest further.

Gabriela, awakened by the ringing phone and the sound of Jamie's voice, popped her head into the room. "Is Max okay? What's going on?"

"Gee hurt her ankle and Boo is sick. Bad headache. There's something they're not telling me. I'll charter a flight home. You can go back to bed."

"No way. I'm coming with you. Give me five minutes, tops."

"Gabriela, it's okay, I'm sure everyone will be fine. I just need to check it out myself."

"Are you kidding? No way am I letting you go by yourself. Plus I am not missing a chance to meet this Boo Charming."

Gabriela grabbed her go bag and stuffed a few pieces of clothing inside. She put on the outfit she had worn to dinner mere hours earlier and called for car service.

Jamie phoned the airport VIP concierge to arrange a private flight. It would be expensive, but Jamie wanted to fly directly into Crestwood's small airstrip to save time.

"Car will be here in a couple of minutes. Ready?" Gabriela asked, bag in hand.

"Let's go," Jamie replied, relieved her best friend was coming with her.

• • • •

IN THE ER, GEE WAS being examined and prepped for an x-ray. Sarah stayed with her daughter as Bryan explained the night's events to the other parents. The other girls were checked out and released into their parents' care. Both apologized and sounded remorseful for sneaking out of the house. It was not clear if the girls realized this was a bad idea from the start or if they were simply sorry Gee was hurt and they were caught.

As soon as Chief pulled up to the ER entrance, Boo was lifted out of the car onto a stretcher. Lessa rushed to Boo's side.

"Thanks, Lessa," Chief called as she returned to her car. "I need to park and pass Fred off to one of my deputies, then I'll be right in."

Boo's brain pounded in her skull. Sitting up made her dizzy. Even when lying on her back, the world did a slow twirl. She was vaguely aware of Lessa taking a hold of her hand as they rolled into an examination room.

"It's good to see you, Boo Charming, but I think we need to stop meeting like this." The attending nurse was the same as Boo's first hospital trip. "This is not a buy three get one free deal."

Ordinarily Boo would have joined in the light banter, but the feelings of nausea kept her silent.

"Do you know what day it is?" the nurse asked.

"Sunday? Maybe Monday now," Boo answered.

"Do you know where you are?"

"Crestwood hospital. Again."

"Do you know who the president is?"

"Obama. Don't wreck my bliss." Boo wanted to laugh but couldn't.

"Okay." The nurse seemed satisfied.

"How are Gee and the girls?" Boo expressed concern even though every word pained her.

"The girls are fine and Gee will be okay," Lessa answered from the end of the bed as the nurse continued her examination of Boo. "They are taking an x-ray of her ankle. Hopefully it's just sprained really badly. I'm sure she'll be on crutches for a while. Crutches will be the least of her worries once Sarah decides on her punishment. I think both kids will be grounded for life now."

"Where's Marco?"

"He's at our house with his Grandpa Philip. Max and Marco are both sleeping through this."

Chief walked in and stood next to Lessa.

"Has anyone called Jamie?" Chief asked.

It was now after three o'clock in the morning.

"Yes, I called when I found out both Gee and Boo were hurt," Lessa replied. "She's on her way home."

"No," Boo protested weakly. "She doesn't have to—"

"Really? Do you know my daughter? Gee being hurt would probably be enough to bring her home, but Gee will be okay. My dear, she will be here for you. In a few short hours."

Boo tried to the nod her relief but the pain in her head stopped her. The sedative in IV drip kicked in and she drifted quietly off to sleep.

• • • •

DANI'S PHONE RANG IN the middle of the night. Still half asleep, she picked up the cellphone and saw the number of the police beat reporter flash on her screen. A call in the middle of the night was never good. Hopefully it was not something gruesome.

"Dani? Been listening to the police scanner. Heard a call out to the Jordan family farm. Several officers. An ambulance. Not sure what's going on. Sounds like a missing persons. I'll let you take this one if you want it."

"Thanks, Rob, I'm on it. I appreciate the call. I'll put you in the byline if there's a story." Dani was grateful to her colleague for calling. He might be giving up a big story. On the other hand, he might simply want to stay in bed and not chase a story in the middle of the night that could turn out to be nothing newsworthy. Either way, Dani jumped out of bed and dressed. Dani's wife, accustomed to middle-of-the-night calls, rolled over to resume sleep.

Dani switched on her scanner in time to hear the ambulance call to the hospital. *One on board and three or four additional incoming.* She thought it unusual for an ambulance crew to not have a firm count of patients. This was enough to justify a quick trip over to the hospital. Dani poured cold coffee in a travel mug and grabbed her car keys.

Fifteen minutes later, Dani stepped inside the ER waiting room. She saw Bryan huddled with two other families. He looked a lot worse for wear, with scratches on his arms and a bandage on one side of his forehead. His clothes were dirty and sweaty.

Dani stepped off to the side of the waiting room and sat down to begin typing a short story on her phone.

Catching sight of Dani, Bryan came over to sit in a chair next to her. He understood the media game—if he gave her enough information for a good story, Dani would not pry further.

"Is everything okay, Bryan? That's as a friend, not a reporter." Dani put the personal concern up front to reinforce her intention to respect the family's privacy.

"Yes, everyone will be fine, thanks for asking. Here's the short version for your story. Three young girls became lost during a night time walk on the Jordan family farm. They were quickly found by an unnamed person during a search. Gee Jordan-Dirk had fallen and was brought to the hospital with an ankle injury. She will be fine. I can't speak for the other girls' families. You'll have to ask them if they want to comment. Is that enough?"

"Thanks, Bryan. Who is the unnamed person? Is that the fourth person brought to the hospital?"

"I cannot give you any information about that person since I am not authorized to speak on their behalf."

Dani put her phone down, indicating she was no longer taking notes and they were off the record now. "Is it the famous Boo Charming?"

"Yes, but I didn't say it and please don't report it. I really can't speak for her. She and Fred did find them and she saved Gee."

"Can I use the part about Fred?" Dani could picture the big fluffy Newfoundland coming to the rescue.

Bryan nodded his consent. Fred would divert attention from Boo.

"Alright, I'll finesse this. Maybe Chief will fill in a bit more."

Bryan nodded his appreciation and left to join Sarah and Gee. Dani continued writing her story until Chief appeared through the ER doors several minutes later. Dani stopped her.

"Bryan told me three young girls were lost on a night time walk at the farm. Gee fell, hurt her ankle, and was brought to the hospital. The person who found the girls is unnamed, but Fred led the way. That should hook everyone's interest. Any comment?"

Chief took a deep breath, composing her thoughts. It was clear that Dani was writing the story because the incident involved the Jordan family.

"Dani, I appreciate you being here at this early hour. Yes, the police were called to the Jordan family farm. We initiated a search for three missing girls. They were found in less than an hour. Two of the girls were checked out and released. One is still in the hospital. I cannot give you names for privacy reasons."

"And the person who found them?"

"That person was also brought to the hospital, although I cannot update you on their condition."

"Thanks, Chief. I'll try to make it a routine story. But, someday, I want to write a feature on this Boo Charming. She's turning into quite a character."

• • • •

THE TRIP TO THE NEW York City airport was quick in the light, pre-dawn traffic. Jamie and Gabriela were dropped off at the entrance to a private executive jet service. The company had a non-disclosure agreement with Jamie's talent agency, minimizing the chance there would be a leak to the press. Fortunately one of the flight crews had arrived early for a flight that was cancelled at the last minute. With the contract signed and new flight plan directly into Crestwood prepared and filed, Jamie and Gabriela boarded the small plane.

"Unless we hit turbulence in this little thing, I am not complaining about flying private." Gabriela appreciated the luxury even under the dire circumstances.

"I need to make a few calls while we're in the air. Would you mind booking your return trip online. Here's my credit card. I really do appreciate you coming with me. I just..." Jamie's voice trailed off. She couldn't explain, even to her longtime friend, her intense need to see Boo and take care of her.

Chapter Twelve

BOO WAS MOVED FROM the ER to a private room for further observation. As promised, Lessa did not leave her side except for a few minutes to check on Gee and Sarah.

Sitting at Boo's bedside, Lessa sipped a cup of tea while absent mindedly picking at a blueberry muffin Bryan brought her. She contemplated the sleeping woman whose bedside she gladly kept watch over. This person had obviously captured the heart of one of her daughters. Her other, not-so-smitten daughter, now owed the two-time hero an apology.

Lessa's phone vibrated.

"Hi, Mom. Where are you?"

"I'm with Boo. She asked for you a couple of times. And about Max. She's sleeping now. The doctors think it's a post-concussion headache. They said it's normal to have severe headaches and dizziness for several weeks after a concussion."

"Thanks for being there with her. How's Gee?"

"She's fine. They will keep her in the hospital until her regular pediatrician can stop by. The x-ray showed a broken bone in her ankle. Nothing requiring surgery, thankfully. She'll have a boot and be on crutches the rest of the summer. While she's grounded."

"We're in the air now and should be there soon. Gabriela is with me. Chief will pick us up at the airport. Said she had a couple hours of comp time coming. Now, will you please tell me what the heck is going on? I want the whole story. Don't spare me any details."

Lessa relayed to Jamie as much as she knew from talking to Bryan, Chief, Sarah, and Gee. Gee swore Boo jumped twenty feet down off the cliff, fought off a den of poisonous snakes, and saved her from certain death. Chief's version was slightly less dramatic and a lot less exaggerated. However, the basic facts were the same—Fred and Boo found and rescued the girls while everyone else was off searching in the opposite direction.

"Wow," Jamie said, taking it all in. "Do you think Sarah might lay off Boo now?"

"I would bet she will. Your big sister is very protective of you." Lessa did not tell Jamie of her plan to have a mother-daughter heart-to-heart with Sarah the minute they were all safely home. Lessa did not like having her daughters at odds and was impatient with Sarah's irrational concerns about Boo. As far as Lessa was concerned, Boo was part of the family.

"What we need to do is add Boo to our health insurance plan as soon as possible. Throwing herself in front of trucks and off cliffs to save our family has turned into a full time job." Jamie shook her head with frustration that her family seemed to be in need of saving on a regular basis and Boo was being harmed in the process. "We should be there by nine. Love you, Mom."

• • • •

CHIEF MET JAMIE AND Gabriela at the small Crestwood airstrip. She was dressed in a deep navy sheriff's department T-shirt and khaki cargo shorts that showed off her toned butt. In the rush home, Jamie had forgotten until now that Gabriela and Chief hooked up during Gabriela's last visit to Crestwood.

"Thanks. I really appreciate this." Jamie hugged Chief, holding on for an extra second to steady her nerves.

"Of course." Chief looked to Gabriela, containing her smile, "It's good to see you, Gabriela. I wish the circumstances were different, but I'm glad you're here." Looking back to Jamie, Chief added, "We have Fred at the police station right now. I didn't have time to drop her back at your house. Shon said they would pick her up later after they found out what you need. I'm pretty sure Fred is being treated quite well at the station, especially since Boo gave her all the credit for tracking down the girls. We may have to deputize them both."

"I'm sure Fred is enjoying the attention. Any updates for me? I talked with Mom before we landed."

"Let's drive you two over to the hospital. I'll fill you in on the way. Gabriela, if you need anything while you're here, please do not hesitate to contact me," Chief spoke in a matter of fact tone, almost covering up the sparks of attraction crackling in the air.

On the short drive from the airstrip to the hospital, Chief recounted the story of the rescue, adding a couple of new details but leaving out the part about Sarah confronting and threatening Boo. That would have to come out later.

At the hospital, Jamie walked directly to Boo's room, finding her sleeping. Lessa pulled her daughter into a comforting embrace. Jamie then sent her mother home to eat and sleep. Lessa stopped long enough in the hallway to warmly greet Gabriela and invite her to the house.

Jamie laid her hand over Boo's, leaning over the raised bed rail carefully to kiss Boo's forehead.

Gabriela watched from the doorway, recognizing the tenderness in this gesture for what it was—the beginning of a great love story. She was pleased by her friend's good fortune but then checked herself, remembering Boo was most likely a married woman. Hopefully her friend would not suffer unrequited love at the end of this seemingly fairy tale romance, complete with a dashing hero and daring rescues.

Jamie joined Gabriela in the doorway to the room. "Mom said that Boo was awake earlier but still had a headache. I want to be here when she wakes up again, so I'm going to find Gee and Sarah now while she's sleeping. Would you mind hanging out here for a few minutes? Can I bring you anything?"

"I'm good. Go."

The room was cool and dark. Gabriela could barely make out Boo's facial features and the rest of Boo's body was covered by a sheet, with her right ankle sticking out, elevated on a pillow. Gabriela stood beside the bed, studying the woman who had captured Jamie's heart. She could see the appeal.

Gabriela reached out to cover Boo's hand with hers and spoke to her in a low voice, "Porbrecita, we're here now. Todo estará bien."

To Gabriela's surprise, Boo squeezed her fingers but did not open her eyes.

"María?" Boo's voice was hoarse, "María, sabía que me encontrarías. I've been waiting for you. Te amo." Boo relaxed into a serene look as she drifted back to sleep.

Not sure what to do, Gabriela remained standing next to the bed, holding Boo's hand until Jamie returned twenty minutes later.

"Jamie, who's María? Is she the possible wife you told me about? When I said something to Boo in Spanish, she thought I was María."

"What exactly did she say?" Jamie's heart sank before she caught the self-pity and straightened up her shoulders.

Gabriela recounted the short, mostly one-sided conversation to Jamie, watching as her friend managed her emotions at the news of Boo declaring love for another woman.

"She might be disappointed when she finds out it was me and not María standing here holding her hand."

"If I know Boo, she'll be very gracious and happy to make your acquaintance. I want to stay here. Go on over to my parents' house and rest. Max is there. He will be thrilled to see his Godma Gabby. There are plenty of people around to take you wherever you want to go or take you out to the farm. You have my code."

"Update me." Gabriela gave her friend a loving squeeze and kiss on the cheek.

Jamie returned to Boo's bedside, lightly stroked Boo's hair. She resolved out loud, "We will find your María Garcia. Soon."

• • • •

DANI POSTED A SHORT story on the Crestwood newspaper's website by six in the morning. The non-sensational story contained a few basic facts about the events of the early morning search and rescue. She obtained permission to include a photo of Fred, portraying her as the hero of the story. Dani thought it made good reading for residents of Crestwood and provided something of mild interest for Jamie's fans.

A few major news outlets quickly picked up the story and re-posted it. The picture of Fred sent it viral within a couple of hours. It seemed that everyone loves a good dog story, especially when coupled with celebrity and the rescue of a child.

A paparazzi who was in Fairfield for a big rock concert the night before, decided it was worth the drive to Crestwood to see if he could sniff out anything juicier on this trip than a couple of drunk kids crashing the stage and throwing up during final song of the night. A new picture of the heroic dog might sell.

As the paparazzi drove into the hospital parking lot mid-morning, he spotted Jamie in the front seat of a car pulling around to the back of the hospital grounds. Grabbing his camera, he skirted the perimeter of the building to shoot a picture of Jamie as she emerged from the car and rushed into the hospital through the service entrance. It looked like she had been up all night. The photo was dramatic enough to sell. He added a pithy caption and uploaded it to some possible news sites to see if they were interested. A quick payment later, he was back in the car looking for breakfast in this small, sleepy town. He might do some more digging later, but at least his trip was paid for.

• • • •

JAMIE WAS NEARLY ASLEEP in the dark hospital room, still holding Boo's hand, when Shon's voice startled her awake. She stepped just outside the room to avoid waking Boo as she talked to Shon.

Shon handed Jamie some comfortable clothes to change into since those in her luggage were what she called her *big city work clothes*. They had also cancelled Jamie's scheduled meetings and talked with her agent.

"Your agent," Shon said the title with more than a little disdain in their voice, "wants you to call. Just a heads up, Dani's story with the picture of Fred went viral. Then, just a few minutes ago, a picture of you coming into the hospital this morning was posted. I have the photographer's name from the credit and will report it to Chief and hospital security. Just wanted you to be aware, someone was out there watching for you."

"Ugh, I'll keep an eye out. Let everyone else know, too. Would you mind picking up Fred at the police station before you head back to the office? And Gabriela is at my parent's. She might need a ride somewhere. Unless Chief is taking care of that."

Shon raised an eyebrow at the last comment, then left for Lessa and Philip's house to check in before retrieving Fred and heading out of town.

From the doorway, Jamie looked back in the room, making sure Boo was still asleep. She fished the work cell phone out of her bag and pressed the speed dial for her agent.

"I suppose you saw the news this morning?" Jamie inquired as soon as her agent answered.

"Yes. How's Gee?"

"Good. We're all still at the hospital. Shon called and cancelled my appointments. We can re-schedule later."

"Jamie, is there something you want to tell me?" This was her agent's line of invitation when he expected bad news.

"No, it's just a family thing."

"Okay. The voice-over gig is on a timeline so you will probably be cut from that. I'll try to save the commercial. They have more lead time. Keep me informed of your schedule. And try to stay away from the paparazzi. If they smell blood, they'll swarm."

The gruesome visual was all too true.

Jamie returned to Boo's room to find her awake, attempting to sit up. Jamie rushed to the bed to steady the patient.

"No, don't sit up. Let's call the nurse first to make sure it's okay."

The nurse who responded to the call light adjusted the bed slowly, raising Boo's upper body into a near sitting position. Boo drank some water and juice. She tried to assure both the nurse and Jamie that her head felt better and she was much less dizzy, but the room still looked wavy from her seated position.

The room was dark except for the light from the hallway, which illuminated the fresh damage to Boo's body—a few scratches and scrapes, and a swollen ankle.

"I can't leave you for a minute, can I?" Jamie's expression was a mixture of affection and deep concern.

"I'm sorry. You didn't need to come back. I heard Gee will be okay. I'm fine. Everyone is taking such good care of me. Your mother was right here with me."

"You're fine? Really? You don't look fine. You looked like something the dog dragged in—literally."

"Fred is an amazing puppy. I'm glad she found the kids as quickly as she did." Boo paused for a moment, her face lighting up. "I had a dream María was here. It seemed so real. I could feel her hand on mine." There were tears in Boo's eyes.

"Someone was here but I'm afraid it was not María. It was my friend, Gabriela. She came home with me and stayed with you for a few minutes while I checked on Gee. She said you called her María, that you knew she would find you, you were waiting for her, and you love her."

"Okay..." Boo wiped away a fallen tear, "hopefully Gabriela was not offended by my declaration of love. I usually don't say that to someone until I've known them for a while. Like, at least the second date."

"Good to know." Jamie made a mental note.

"When can I meet Gabriela, for real?"

"As soon as you feel better and we take you home, then we'll make a proper introduction. I'm sure you'll still te amo her. Everyone does."

Chapter Thirteen

THE ROOM WAS DARK EVEN though it was a sunny mid-afternoon in early June. The opaque shades were drawn closed. Heavy breathing was the language of two people negotiating their lustful intentions toward each other. The rustle of clothes being removed and discarded was punctuated by the sounds of lips coming together and apart, at first slowly, then with more intensity. A low hum, the electricity of attraction and desire, built in the air.

The room was cool but sweat began to form as skin slid over skin. The increasing friction took on an urgency neither woman wanted nor had the willpower to stop. In the dark it was hard to tell where one body ended and the other began.

A phone rang. Something beeped. The door was locked and anyone looking for them would have to knock to gain entry to this momentary sanctuary.

As a tongue slipped from mouth to neck to nipple, murmurs of encouragement were barely audible between hard breaths. Fingers ran through soft hair. Hands traced lean shoulders and clutched at the muscled back of the woman kissing her way down the stomach of her paramour. The murmurs became moans.

Any thought of extending this moment quickly gave way to the tension created by their mutual desire. There would be time later for a more careful exploration. This time was about immediate cause and effect. A gentle bite here earns a moan. A finger flick there causes a sharp intake of breath. A lick along this spot sends ripples through the body. Putting them all together equals rolling waves of pleasure suspending a brief moment in time.

• • • •

AFTER AN EARLY LUNCH, Shon and Bryan retrieved Fred from the police station. Shon's bright yellow car was barely large enough for two adults. Fred inhabited the back seat as if it were her throne, sticking her head first out one window, then the other as they drove away from the station.

Seemingly the entire town had read Dani's story of Fred's heroic actions. People waved, shouted, and applauded as the yellow chariot with a brave giant head sticking out the window drove by on a slow tour of Main Street. Fred,

Shon, and Bryan enjoyed the processional so much that they decided to take a second lap through town. They also hoped if a paparazzi was still around, this photo op would satisfy the urge to click and send him on his way.

Once back at the farm, Shon dropped Bryan off at Jamie's house to drive her SUV back to the hospital. At the office, Shon spent the afternoon reading messages to Fred from her fandom. The story of Fred was viral on several media platforms and people were posting adoring tributes and stories of their own dog's heroic feats.

"Here's a good one from Nova Scotia. Looks just like you. Says she saved a small child who fell off a boat while fishing in the bay. Jumped right in, plucked the boy out of the icy waters, and took him back to the boat. Then swam a mile to shore." Shon scratched and patted Fred's head. "Aren't you glad we just make you walk through snake and tick infested woods? You may land a movie deal out of this, you big lovable lug."

Fred had stolen the spotlight, which was fine with Shon. As long as the positive spin continued, there would be less social media management to do. Shon thought a good strategy for diverting attention from Boo would be to talk Jamie into allowing Dani to write a feature story on Fred, the rescue wonder dog.

• • • •

BOO SPENT THE AFTERNOON recovering at the hospital. The doctor would clear Boo to leave as soon as she could stand and walk without feeling dizzy. Her headache had subsided, but she was cautioned against encounters with bright lights and loud noises for the next few days.

Across town at her parent's house, Jamie ate a late lunch with Max, who was excited about the idea of spending time with his Godma Gabby. Between his Godma's unexpected visit and his grandparents' loving attention, Max did not seem to miss his mother, leaving her with a twinge of sadness. Jamie rang Gabriela's cell and left a message updating her. Chief had taken Gabriela to lunch and they had yet to reappear.

"As soon as Bryan brings my car, I'll take Boo home. Would you two mind keeping Max for one more night? Gabriela will probably stay here with him."

"Of course we'll keep Max." Philip affectionately ran a hand over his grandson's head. "Marco is also staying tonight, while Gee gets settled at home. Would you send Gabriela a text and tell her dinner is at 6:00? She and Chief can join us."

Jamie texted Gabriela the invitation. Still no reply.

After a few moments of quiet time, Lessa drove her daughter to the hospital.

"How are you holding up, honey? You haven't had much sleep and it was a quick trip."

"I'm glad I came home and that Gabriela is with me. We really need to find this María Garcia. She's the most concrete clue we have to Boo's identity." Jamie looked at her mother for reassurance as she formed a new resolve. "I think it's time I tell Boo who I am."

"Boo already knows who you are, but I'm sure she will appreciate hearing more about your life. She is obviously attached to you in lots of ways. And you to her." Lessa was only slightly coy with her words. "Chief said something about it being time to post something on the internet, maybe a picture of Boo as a missing person, but she's afraid it will bring out the scammers."

"I was thinking, after I tell Boo about my work maybe we could make a public appearance together. As friends. Then her picture would be posted without saying we are searching for her identity. If someone is looking for her they would try to contact her or us. What do you think?"

"Sounds like a good idea to me. Do you want something low-key here in town? There's a local art exhibit opening Thursday night. We could go as a family, that way we could shield her from too much attention. We can tip Dani off and make sure there's a camera crew there."

"Sounds great. I'll talk to Boo and Chief before we make final plans." Jamie's thoughts were back on the deception by omission she needed to clear up with Boo. "I hope my talk with Boo goes as planned and she's not angry with me."

"Oh, honey, I'm sure she'll understand. She loves the real you. You're the same person she has learned to rely on."

Lessa had intentionally used the word *love*. The word both comforted and scared Jamie.

• • • •

GABRIELA AND CHIEF showered in separate bathrooms at Chief's house to avoid being any later for dinner than they already were. Chief tried to decide which would look less guilty of the afternoon tryst—making an excuse to bow out of dinner, or showing up with a silly grin on her face. Given that very little escaped Lessa's notice, she decided she might as well join her friends and enjoy the dinner.

Gabriela checked her cell phone. Two missed calls and several text messages from Jamie. She texted back that she was on her way to dinner at Jamie's parents' house and would stay there with Max for the night. Gabriela knew Jamie would figure out the reason for her afternoon disappearance as soon as she was less distracted by Boo's health scare.

• • • •

BRYAN DROVE JAMIE'S car to the back of the hospital, maneuvering behind a delivery truck to obscure the direct line of sight from outside the immediate loading dock area. Hopefully this would prevent any more paparazzi pictures from surfacing later. Finding Jamie outside Boo's room, he gave her the keys and a hug, and left to retrieve his own car to take Gee and Sarah home.

Boo waited in the room, sunglasses on even though the room was dark. She walked slowly but steadily beside Jamie, still limping on her sore ankle.

"The car is out back. Do you need anything before we leave town?" Jamie wanted to take hold of Boo's arm but allowed Boo to walk out on her own.

"I can't think of anything. You really didn't have to come home. I feel bad you missed your work obligations."

Jamie stopped in her tracks, turning to look directly at Boo. "I came home because I would have been too worried about you and Gee to be effective at work anyway. It is far more important to me to be here, with you, and Gee and Sarah. I am right where I am supposed to be. Now, do you want ice cream before we leave town or not?"

"Chocolate fudge, please?" Boo had learned that arguing with a resolute Jamie was futile.

Jamie helped Boo into the SUV, driving slowly out of the service area while scanning the parking lot for possible paparazzi. She planned to have a long talk with Boo as soon as they were settled at home. Jamie was pre-occupied by how to begin the conversation. *A good script would come in handy about now*, she mused.

The trip home was mostly silent. Boo licked her ice cream cone deliberately to keep the drips from escaping onto her clothes or the car seats. She closed her eyes against the bright sunshine. Sensing Jamie's distracted mood, Boo did not want to pry.

At home, Jamie fixed a light dinner in the kitchen, closing the blinds and dimming the lights. It gave dinner an unintended romantic ambience.

"Boo, we need to talk. First, I want to be clear that I am committed to finding María Garcia and I have a plan." Jamie paused to gather her thoughts. "There's a story that goes with this plan that I need to explain first. I haven't been totally forthcoming about my work. I act...in movies mostly. I have for almost twenty years. I have no idea if you would have seen any of my films. It's been a very lucrative career for me, and means that a lot of people recognize me."

"Should I recognize you? I'm sorry if I—"

"No, you would not necessarily recognize me. And, you do know who I am—Jamie Jordan. Mom. Chauffeur. Great cook—don't you dare disagree with the last part." Jamie winked at Boo. "You just know me here at home, not when I'm at work."

"What kind of movies are you in? Would I have seen them?"

"If you want, we could watch parts of a couple of movies later. See if you recognize something." Jamie was relieved the new information apparently did not trigger recognition of her career.

"If you want to show me, that's great, but it's not necessary. I respect your privacy and if you don't want to talk about your work, it's okay." Boo still did not grasp the extent of Jamie's fame or the lack of privacy Jamie had in her life because of her work.

"The other thing I need to tell you is that some people do not respect my privacy. They think all of my life should be available to the public. This includes people who make a living by taking pictures or finding stories about people like me mostly doing ordinary things. It's an unfortunate consequence of my job and sometimes makes it difficult for me to do things with other people without it being reported like it's big news. It has caused me to be distrustful of new people."

The last sentence hit Boo, shaking her sense of ease with Jamie.

"I can leave. I don't want to make you uncomfortable, especially in your own home. I'm not here..." She wasn't here by choice exactly, although she had needed a place to stay and Jamie seemed to have freely invited her.

"Boo, this is not about you. I want you here. I enjoy having you here. I feel comfortable around you. In fact, I have probably taken advantage of you not knowing about my career and I am sorry for that. I think maybe I have kept you somewhat isolated so I could keep you all to myself." It felt cathartic and scary to Jamie to reveal her true feelings.

"I'm confused. Why are you telling me this now?"

"A couple of reasons. First, there was a picture online of me arriving at the hospital this morning, which means there is a paparazzi looking for pictures to make some money. So, if you are with me, your picture could be posted anytime."

"Okay. Is that bad?"

"Not necessarily, and in fact it plays into my plan for finding out your identity. My mother told me there's an art show opening in town on Thursday. It's just a local show, but if you show up with me, there will be pictures, and those pictures will be posted online. Although you will be attending as a friend of the family, some people will speculate that you and I might be dating. If people think I might be dating someone new, it tends to go viral." In Jamie's mind it sounded innocent, but when she said it out loud she realized how much the plan reflected her true desire—to be with Boo as more than just a friend.

"Are you sure people will take pictures?"

"Oh, trust me, they will. Most local people don't care because they have known me since I was a child, but some people can't resist. Plus, we'll tip off one of the local reporters. It's an efficient way for a lot of people to see your picture. We think someone might recognize you and try to contact you, especially if they have been looking for you. If not, we'll move to Plan B."

"What's Plan B?"

"I'm not sure yet. We'll figure it out if we have to. This just seems way better than Chief posting your mug shot on a milk carton. That brings out the whacko's. This is a different kind of crazy."

"Okay. If you think this is a good plan," Boo put on her best brave look. "Will Shon dress me for my big debut?"

"I am sure they will love this assignment."

Chapter Fourteen

AFTER DINNER, JAMIE and Boo settled next to each other on the sofa in the TV room. Fred, who had not left Boo's side since she returned home, was at their feet.

Jamie dimmed the lights, lowered the brightness level of the TV screen, and found three of her movies to stream. Not wanting to overload Boo with loud yelling or flashing quick-cut images, Jamie picked a couple of popular, light-hearted comedies that had success in the theaters and been shown on TV several times. If Boo were to have seen any of her films, these would be the most likely candidates. After watching ten minutes of each, with Jamie's characters prominently on screen, Boo showed no recognition.

"That's really amazing how you can change your whole persona. Did you study acting?"

"Lots of study and lots of on the job training." Jamie remained humble about her skills.

Next, Jamie choose an animated film where she voiced one of the characters.

"I recognize this movie." Boo closed her eyes to listen to the movie dialogue. "Is that your voice? It doesn't sound much like you."

"I'm the bear's voice. I'm surprised you recognize—hey, are you saying I sound like a bear?" Jamie teased Boo, remembering how hard she worked to create a voice unrecognizable as her own.

"No, you don't sound like a bear—much," Boo dead-panned her reply. "I remember the movie. I took my nephew when he was little."

"Okay, well, we seem to have found your genre of choice. Let's try this one." Jamie streamed another animated film where she performed the voice of a dolphin.

"I remember this one, too. I must have the movie taste of a five-year-old." Boo was excited by the discovery. "Should I have known who you are from these movies?"

"Unless you read the credits, there's no reason you would connect the movie character to my voice." Jamie felt oddly relieved the movies Boo recognized were not movies where she appeared in character. "Shall we call it a night?

I don't want to disobey doctor's orders. We don't want your headache to come back."

"I am tired...why didn't you tell me before?" Boo's face held a mixture of hurt and curiosity, trying to understand if Jamie thought she was a bad person who was out to hurt her.

"I guess I've just had lots of bad experiences with people wanting to be close to me for the celebrity of it. I learned to not trust people. It's been nice to meet someone with no expectations or preconceptions. It was selfish of me. I am truly sorry if I hurt you."

"No, I understand...I think...I mean, I can't really understand what it's like for you, but you certainly need to protect yourself, and Max and your family. Is this why Sarah doesn't want me around? She thinks I want to use you?"

"Yes. She'll come around."

Boo took Jamie's hand in hers and slowly raised it to her lips for a kiss. The whole evening had been unintentionally romantic. The atmosphere, with the lights dimmed and sitting next to each other, created an amorous closeness. Boo's gesture was intended to be reassuring, but given her track record as Boo Charming, it's effect was more lovingly tender than chivalrous.

Neither woman wanted to part for the night, but both were certain that they must.

· · · ·

EARLY THE NEXT MORNING, Boo wandered into the kitchen where Jamie was making breakfast. While Boo had slept through the night, mostly due to sheer exhaustion, Jamie tossed and turned all night wondering if she had done the right thing, if this was the right time, and what would happen next. Jamie exhausted herself with what-if's.

"Good morning. How did you sleep?" Jamie inquired.

"I slept well, thank you. And you?" Boo noticed the careful politeness with which they were approaching each other.

"A little restless," Jamie shaded the truth. "Breakfast?"

"Yes."

"Would you like a hug with that? You know, since Max isn't around for the morning honors." Jamie tried to make it seem like she was a mere stand-in, though she offered more for her own desire to hold Boo than as a substitute for Max.

Boo slipped her arms around Jamie's shoulders, who reciprocated with an embrace of Boo's waist. The contact generated a heat that threatened to catch fire. They stood in the embrace for a long minute until Jamie smelled a bagel burning in the toaster.

"We better not set the house on fire. It would be embarrassing if we had to call the fire department." Jamie forced herself to step away from Boo.

"Or, if I end up back in the ER because I tried to save you." Boo leaned against the kitchen counter, breathing in the scent of Jamie's body lingering in the air between them. "Are you sorry you told me?"

"No, I'm glad I told you. I'm just scared that things might change." Jamie paused to consider whether she was being over-dramatic. "Things will change. That's the whole point of finding your identity, finding María, and your home. Plus, eventually I will have to start a new project, and probably leave for a while for a job. I think I'm just being selfish. You're the first person to come into my life in a long time..." Jamie could not think how to finish the sentence gracefully.

"Shall we change the subject, for now?"

"Yes, please." Jamie brought bagels and fruit to the table, reciting the plans for the day, "Gabriela and Max will arrive soon. We'll ask Shon to work on finding clothes for you for the gallery opening. Shon and my mother will make some calls to the press. We like to support the local arts so this will all look normal."

"What can I do?"

"How about you take it easy? Hopefully, no one will need saving today." Jamie turned her attention to the morning newspaper.

Boo stared out the window, feeling more optimistic than she had in a while that she would soon learn her identity. After the breakfast table was cleared, Boo stepped out on the patio. She enjoyed the fresh morning air before the sun became too bright. She closed her eyes and took long deep breaths to clear her mind.

A few minutes later, Jamie placed two cups of tea on the patio table and joined Boo to take in the light blue of the dawn sky. Slipping an arm around Boo's waist, Jamie pulled Boo close to her.

Boo looked at Jamie. It had not occurred to her before, but she could see the movie star beauty in the soft strength of Jamie's face. All Boo had focused on before last night was the warm, caring person who was generous beyond measure. The woman she had grown to love was still standing here in front of her.

Leaning in, Boo kissed the top of Jamie's forehead. She closed her eyes and left her lips pressed against Jamie's soft skin.

"I really want to kiss you." Jamie had the thought many times, but this was the first time she voiced it out loud.

"Mmmm, me too," Boo's words reverberated from her lips against Jamie's skin, "but I don't want to hurt you. I don't want to find out...I can't..." The sentence was left suspended before Boo could add what she truly wanted to say, "*before I fall in love with you.*"

The moment was interrupted by the sound of Sarah's car approaching.

• • • •

AT THE EDGE OF THE woods, two eyes watched the women in their intimate embrace.

• • • •

JAMIE AND BOO WERE in the kitchen by the time Sarah let herself in the front door.

"Don't you knock?" Jamie glared at her sister. Lessa had told her about Sarah's actions, accusing Boo of a heinous act. She was also annoyed that her sister interrupted an intimate moment with Boo.

"How's Gee?" Boo asked the question to break the tense standoff between the sisters by focusing on important concerns.

"Gee's fine, thanks to you. We promised her she would see you today. She wants to thank you herself." Sarah looked down as an uncomfortable silence enveloped the kitchen. "I need to apologize, Boo, I have treated you unfairly."

"Really? You think?" Jamie could not resist interjecting her indignation against her sister.

"Please, I do not want you two to fight anymore." Boo needed to put an end to the sister drama.

"No, it's okay. Jamie has every right to be angry with me. And so do you, Boo. I have acted deplorably. I rushed to judgment about you. I was scared but that is no excuse." Sarah words were deliberate and heartfelt. "I will not ask you to forgive me. I will have to earn your trust."

"I very much appreciate what you just said." Boo ignored Jamie's look of disbelief and addressed Sarah directly, "It means a lot to me. I'm glad we can move forward from here. Jamie told me some about why you worry. I appreciate you were scared and I hope I have earned your trust."

"You have. Thank you for finding Gee and her friends. God knows what would have happened if you had not found them when you did. You put yourself in a lot of danger out there."

"Well, I couldn't have done it without Fred." Boo scratched the big dog's head.

Fred had quietly entered the room when Sarah came in. She must have remembered the last encounter between Sarah and Boo because she sat down at Boo's side to monitor the proceedings.

"Would you please join us for family dinner this evening?" Sarah looked to Jamie. "And you and Max and Gabriela, too."

Sarah's use of the word family was not lost on Jamie, who softened slightly toward her sister. She was still pissed off, but the hot anger subsided.

"A family meal would be very nice," Jamie reinforced the use of the word *family*. "By the way, I told Boo last night, about my work. No more secrets."

The revelation caught Sarah off-guard but before she could react, Max burst through the front door.

"Boo!" Max ran into Boo's arms.

Gabriela entered the kitchen behind Max. She was met with a warm hug and wet kiss on on both cheeks from Jamie, and customary nose to the crotch from Fred.

"Oh, it's great to be loved. Speaking of which," Gabriela smiled, turning her attention to Boo and extending her hand, "hi, I'm Gabriela. I don't believe we have formally met."

"I'm Boo, although I'm sure you know that since I have already declared my love to you." Boo winked at Gabriela and charmed her with a pleasing grin.

Sarah, confused by what appeared to be Boo openly flirting with Gabriela in front of Jamie, immediately scowled until Jamie broke out laughing. Sarah looked at Jamie out of the corner of her eye.

"I hope you will clear this up for me later?"

"I hope we clear up a lot of things soon," Jamie replied.

Chapter Fifteen

AFTER SHON DROPPED Gabriela and Max at Jamie's house, they immediately reached for their phone.

"Hey Chief. I saw a car parked at the lake this morning. It looks like the same car I spotted cruising past the house a few times yesterday. Maybe someone around here has a new car, but it looks like a rental to me. I thought it might be the paparazzi guy who's been lurking around town."

"Thanks, Shon, I'll check it out." Chief was at the office early catching up on paperwork that had accumulated on her desk while she was indisposed the day before.

Chief grabbed the keys to her Sheriff's car, then changed her mind. Wanting to pay a social visit to Jamie's house after checking out the car at the lake, she made a quick change into civilian clothes and drove her personal car. Chief would not want to be accused of using an official vehicle for a private trip, or her uniform for the purpose of seduction.

Chief arrived at the lake, where a couple of local cars were parked in the main lot. She spotted the car fitting Shon's description pulled off to one side, on the grass under a large tree. The car had a small sticker on the front window indicating it belonged to a rental car company. Chief peered in the driver's side window, seeing several food wrappers, a large cup in the drink holder, and a duffle bag on the floor of the back seat with an airline tag on it.

Chief called the local tow company.

"Hey, Lyle, do you have time right now to drive out to the lake and tow an illegally parked car?...How soon will you be here?"

Chief cited the vehicle for parking in a restricted zone and then dialed the rental car company number to report the tow, as a courtesy in case the customer called to report the car stolen.

Lyle arrived in his truck within fifteen minutes. Dragging the car onto the truck bed for transport took less than ten minutes. Lyle, not the talkative type, hopped into his truck cab to finish the intake sheet for the city impound lot.

"Thanks Lyle. I'll wait for a few minutes to see if this person shows up." Chief intended to wait as long as it took.

Lyle grunted his goodbye and pulled out onto the highway toward town.

Invading anyone's privacy made Chief angry. Invading Jamie's privacy made her very angry. She was glad to be in civilian clothes, which would play into her plan.

. . . .

THE CAR IN THE PARKING lot was rented by a paparazzi nicknamed Pops. At forty-nine, in what he called *a young man's game*, Pops was considered old for a paparazzi. There were a few female paparazzi, but mostly it was a blood sport of young men with little or no compassion for others who wanted to make a quick buck. Hence, Pops stood out in the crowd of photographers who inevitably descended on celebrities or the victims of notorious crimes. He derived his nickname from the younger guys who couldn't decide whether to look up to him like a father-figure or push him out of the way.

Pops had been a legitimate news photographer for years, but the layoffs from traditional newspapers and magazines made those jobs scarce. The expense of putting a kid through college and being nowhere near retirement age led Pops to forget his journalistic integrity and hit the streets. After a few lucky shots of a minor celebrity acting badly—throwing a couple of drunken punches at a security guard at a club—sold quickly and easily, he justified this dubious career move to his family and friends as, *If I don't do it, someone will. It might as well be me making the money.*

Pops snapped pictures of Jamie at a couple of movie openings over the years. He liked Jamie because she played nice, posing for the photographers to take their shots. He also had been told that she was *unavailable* for the summer months, between projects and with no public appearances planned.

The news about Jamie's son barely escaping death broke while he was on another assignment, causing him to miss attending the hasty news conference that was non-news anyway. This week he was in Fairfield to cover a concert tour when he saw Dani's story about the dog rescuing Jamie's niece. Smelling money, Pop's added a day in Crestwood to his trip.

After searching public records, Pops used satellite maps to identify Jamie's home. He drove by a couple of times to confirm his research and check out the terrain. He also befriended a local who was more than happy to gossip about the Jordan's. That was where he first heard it was not Fred who saved the girls, but a mysterious stranger living with Jamie. The gossip confirmed recent speculation about Jamie having a new woman in her life. No pictures of this new girlfriend had surfaced yet, which meant money was there for the taking.

Lying in wait for Jamie and the mystery woman to appear in public might take several days. Pops decided to chart a course to get close enough to Jamie's house to take pictures. Even with a long lens, he would have to be within a couple hundred yards to get a shot good enough to sell. That is, if there was a clear line of sight. The satellite view showed a clearing behind Jamie's house. Although it would be tricky, Pops figured if he could make his way to the edge of the clearing, it should be close enough.

Early Tuesday morning was quiet at the lake. Arriving just before the sun peeked over the horizon, Pops tucked his rental car off the side of the parking lot, in the grass where it would be less noticeable. A dozen canoes rested on racks near the boat launch dock.

"Doesn't look like anyone will mind if I borrow one," Pops justified out loud, hoping he would return before anyone else appeared at the lake that morning.

Pops was by no means an expert with a paddle, but the plan was to make his way to the side of the lake where a wide creek went under the highway bridge and wound around to the back side of Jamie's property. There he hoped to find a landing and a path through the woods, leading to the edge of the clearing. If there was no path, it would be tough bushwhacking through the summer undergrowth. He packed water and snack bars, and sprayed himself with insect repellant for what could be a long wait in the woods. Unfortunately he was not wearing snake boots, so he would be taking his chances in that regard.

Paddling down the creek with the current was easy. He navigated his way to a spot which appeared on the map to be closest to the back of Jamie's house. Pops pulled the canoe out of the creek, leaving it on the bank and hoping he could find the creek and canoe again. Otherwise, his Plan B involved announcing his presence and possibly being arrested for trespassing.

"I really need to find an easier job," Pops said, talking to himself as he crawled up the creek bank. "I'm getting too old for this."

"No snakes, no snakes, no snakes," was his mantra as he crashed through the woods until a trail appeared. Three-quarters of a mile along the trail, Pops settled into a spot at the edge of the clearing behind Jamie's house. There was a clear view of the pool and patio and he could see light through the kitchen window. He would have to sell any photos anonymously to avoid being prosecuted for trespassing, but an exclusive photo would bring in big money making it worth the risk.

Pops did not have to wait long. A tall, dark haired woman stepped out on the patio. *Who's that?* he wondered, *definitely not Jamie or anyone from her family*. Soon, Jamie herself appeared next to the mystery woman.

Pops leveled his lens at them, taking six shots to test the light and focus. He checked the photos on the screen on the back of the camera. They were on the dark side and grainy, but a person could tell it was Jamie. She was recognizable.

Just then the women wrapped their arms around each other. It didn't matter who the other woman was now, they were in what could easily be captioned *a lover's embrace*. Dollar signs flashed in Pop's mind as he kept his finger pinned down on the rapidly clicking shutter. *Jackpot!*

A minute later a car approached the house and the might-be lovers left their embrace, disappearing inside the house. Pops waited several minutes. As soon as a second car came toward the house, he started back down the trail towards the creek. Paddling against the current, the return trip to the lake took a lot longer, requiring Pops to use muscles he did not ordinarily use during a workday.

"I could have been a wedding photographer," Pops told himself as he struggled. "Bridezilla must be less dangerous than snakes."

By the time Pops floated to the dock, he was sweating and tired. He pulled the canoe from the lake onto the shore and carried it to the rack. Reorienting himself, he walked past the other cars in the parking lot toward the spot where he left the rental car. There were three fishing boats drifting on the lake, but no one paid any attention to his presence.

"That went well," Pops congratulated himself. He was impatient, wanting to sit in the car and check the pictures to figure out which ones would bring the most money. He would send those choice photos while he waited at the airport for his flight.

• • • •

AS SHE WAITED IN THE parking lot for the towed car's driver, Chief pulled on a floppy fishing hat. Keeping the trunk lid up to hide the badge on the license plate, she tidied her car. During a trip to the recycling bin by the picnic tables, she spotted a man pulling a canoe out of the water. A camera with a long lens hung from his neck. She reasoned this had to be the paparazzi guy.

Chief watched as Pops made his way through the parking lot toward the now empty space where the towed car had been parked. Pops looked around, seeming unsure if he was in the right spot. He turned around twice, looking in every direction.

"Shit...shit, shit, shit," Pops began a new mantra.

"Everything okay?" Chief called over to where Pops was making himself dizzy whirling around.

"Shit. My car's been stolen."

"What did your car look like?" Chief walked toward Pops, her hat pulled low.

"It was gray, 4 doors."

"Ah, must have been your car I saw the tow truck leave with a few minutes ago."

"Shit. Why would they tow it?"

"Did you park there? On the grass?"

"Yes. Why?"

"See the sign over there?" Chief pointed to the *No Parking on the Grass* sign. "They do that all the time. Pisses me off. Had my car towed once, too. They just want your money." Chief was laying it on thick to gain Pop's confidence.

"No shit. Where do they take the car? "

"City impound."

"Guess I need a taxi—is there even a taxi or ride service in this place?"

"Good luck finding a driver who'll come all the way out here. Take an hour, at least."

"Damn. I have a plane to catch." Pops searched his pockets for his cell phone.

"Hey, would you like a ride to town? I'm probably not going to catch anything today anyway. I can drop you off at the impound. It's on my way home."

"Really? That would be great. I'll pay you." Pops wanted to add, *anything to get out of this hell-hole*, but decided to not chance offending a local.

"Ah, no problem. Hate to see people treated bad. In fact, maybe we can catch the driver before he drops the car. Those guys stop at the diner on the north side of town, just hang out. If he's there, bet if you buy his lunch, he'll let you have the car. They don't give a shit where their money comes from," Chief spoke rapid-fire, reeling Pops in.

"Great. Thanks. Let's go."

"Sure, let me grab my reels from the fishing pier over there. Would you mind giving me a hand? I set up four this morning. Don't want to leave 'em out here. They're expensive and some yahoo will come along and steal 'em." Chief walked toward the fishing pier hoping Pops would follow. "Do you want to leave your camera in my car?"

"No, it's fine." Pops scurried alongside his volunteer driver.

Chief was counting on the regulars having left a few rods at the end of the pier. In the summer some of the old fishers would say they were leaving fishing poles for the kids, but really it was just in case they were driving past and wanted to stop and cast a line.

As Chief and Pops reached the long wooden pier, there were indeed four rods lined up on the other end. The poles did not look expensive, but the visual was good enough to keep up the story. Chief proceeded along the pier with Pops beside her. The camera was hanging on Pops' side, the strap slung over one shoulder.

"You one of those nature photographers?" Chief sounded mildly interested.

"Birds mostly." Pops had used the story before even though he knew next to nothing about feathered fowl. If it was red it must be a cardinal, anything blue was a blue jay, and everything else was just something that might leave a mess on his car.

Chief tripped as she neared the end of the pier, bumping into Pops just enough to cause him to lose his balance and lurch off the pier into the water. The water was about five feet deep at the point where Pops belly flopped and submerged. He quickly broke through surface, found his footing to stand, and gasped for air.

"What the fuck? What'd you do that for?" Pops sputtered.

"I'm sorry," Chief did her best contrite look, "I'm so clumsy. Here, let me help you."

Pops grabbed at a plank on the pier to pull himself up but lost his grip and fell back in the water. At that point he gave up and swam toward shore. Emerging from the water, soaked and dripping, disgust enveloped his face as he looked at his dripping camera. He felt his pocket for his phone, which was undoubtedly frying its own insides as he stood there.

Chief looked at him, not bothering to contain a smirk.

Pops instantly flushed red with anger. "You did that on purpose, you—" Pops charged Chief, taking a swing that grazed her chin.

On his follow through, Chief gave Pops a little trip, shoving him to the ground. She stepped back as the soaked paparazzi scrambled to his feet for another charge.

Chief pulled the badge from her back pocket, holding it directly in front of Pops face. "You're under arrest for assaulting a police officer."

Pops halted, eyes focusing on the face in front of him. Chief's hat had come off during the altercation and he recognized her from a picture at one of Jamie's openings. "You're...shit."

Chapter Sixteen

"YOU HAVE THE RIGHT to remain silent. Anything you say can and will be used against you in a court of law. You have the right—" Chief's recitation was interrupted.

"Yeah, yeah, whatever," Pops had illusions of negotiating his way out of this mess. "What do you want?"

"I don't want anything. You were doing okay until you hit me." Chief remained calm, having already achieved most of her objective. "Give me the camera and your phone. You can make a call from the station. What's your name?"

Pops handed over the useless phone but hesitated to give up the camera. When Chief held out her hand, Pops handed her the dripping equipment.

"People call me Pops. You know you can't search either of those without a warrant."

"Of course I know that," Chief smirked, wanting to make Pops uncomfortable. "What were you really taking pictures of? It wasn't birds."

Pops remained silent.

"Okay." Chief pulled out her cell phone and called dispatch, "Send a car out to the lake. I have one to bring in and I don't want him getting my seats wet." Chief ended the call and turned back to Pops. "Do I need to put a twisty tie on your hands or will you behave?"

"And if I don't behave?" Pops inquired smugly.

"I'll shoot you in your bad leg first."

"I don't have a bad leg."

"You will after I shoot you." Chief's chuckle possessed a hint of menace.

Pops nodded his understanding and walked slowly toward the parking lot. Chief followed, slinging the dripping camera over her shoulder.

"Have I seen you before?" Chief asked out of interest more than interrogation.

"I remember you from a movie opening. You worked security."

"Ah, yes. This probably isn't how you planned your day," Chief sounded almost sympathetic. "Were you planning on selling these pictures or were you trespassing just for the heck of it?"

Pops didn't answer. He leaned against Chief's car to wait, still soaked from his dip in the lake.

"If I see a picture anywhere, I will know it's you. Then we'll charge you with trespassing on top of assault." Chief upped the ante in this game.

"I didn't have time to upload any pictures of the love birds, if that's what you're wondering." Pops hoped for some leniency by providing this much information while not confessing to any crimes.

"Good. We'll loan you some dry clothes at the station. Want a granola bar? Bottle of water?" Chief played the benevolent captor. She sensed Pops was telling the truth about not uploading pictures from the camera, but if there were any on the phone, they might be stored on a backup site in the cloud. Chief would ask Shon to keep an eye on social media for new pictures of Jamie, or Boo, that might have originated from someone trespassing. With any luck, this bullet had been dodged. For now.

A uniformed sheriff's deputy arrived several minutes later and loaded Pops in the back of his patrol car.

"Book him on a felony charge of assaulting a police officer and a misdemeanor theft by unlawful taking—let's just say he borrowed a canoe without asking. I'll be in soon to do the paperwork. Do not take him to today's initial appearances at the courthouse. I don't want him out on bail yet. He should have an out-of-state ID. A felony assault will keep him in until tomorrow morning. Understood?"

The deputy nodded his understanding and inquired, "He hit you, Chief?"

"Yes, but I'm okay. Don't be hard on him. He's had a really tough day."

Chief handed the camera to her deputy, turning it on as she let go. They both heard sizzling crackles inside the camera body.

"Oops."

• • • •

AT THE FARM, SHON BUZZED Chief through the gate. Chief stopped by the office first to update Shon and Sarah, summarizing the morning arrest.

"I'm not sure what pictures he took or if he uploaded any. He was down the creek meaning he was out behind the house. I'll talk to Jamie. Keep an eye on social media for any pictures or posts that might come from this guy. I'll see if

I can get a warrant to search the camera and phone, but I doubt a judge will allow it. We may have to play wait and see."

Shon and Sarah both nodded solemnly before Sarah changed the subject.

"Would you join us for family dinner tonight? We'll talk about everything." Sarah would let Jamie inform Chief about her plans to take Boo to the gallery opening.

"Thanks, but I don't want to intrude."

"You're family. Be there at 6:00," Sarah's declaration was a command not easily disobeyed.

As Chief made her way out of the office, Shon called after her in a sing-song voice, "By the way, I dropped Gabriela off at the house a little while ago."

Chief blushed like a child caught with her hand in the cookie jar.

· · · ·

MAX RAN TO THE FRONT door to greet Chief. The enthusiasm of a four-year-old is as refreshing as it is infectious. Jamie and Boo both hugged Chief.

Gabriela was last in the greeting line. She looked Chief over, giving an appreciative smile. As she leaned in to embrace Chief, she whispered, "If I grab your ass, will you have to arrest me for assaulting an officer?"

"Somebody already beat you to it today," Chief wisecracked in response.

Gabriela took a step back, looking at Chief's face for clues about whether she should be jealous or alarmed.

"I need to talk to Jamie." Chief turned to Boo. "Would you excuse us for a few minutes, please."

"Sure. Max and I are working on a get-well card for Gee." Boo looked around for Max, who had already disappeared into his room to retrieve coloring pencils.

"Gabriela can stay. It will save me the time repeating it all." Jamie looked expectantly at Chief.

Chief recounted the morning's events to Jamie and Gabriela, including the arrest for assaulting a police officer, implicitly explaining her reply to Gabriela's earlier proposition.

"Bottom line is we can bet he took pictures. What we don't know is what those pictures were or if any of them will end up posted."

Jamie remembered her tender morning embrace with Boo on the patio. If Sarah had not arrived when she did, there might have been an even more interesting photo op. Her cheeks blushed at the thought.

"Boo and I were on the patio early this morning. It would have been a clear shot from the woods. I remember Fred going down there later and sniffing around. I bet she smelled this guy." Jamie felt violated, as though her safe place had been invaded. "I remember the guy you're talking about. He was always one of the nicer ones. Never tried to bait people. I wouldn't have thought he would sink this low." Jamie was beyond being surprised by what people would do, enticed by the lure of money.

"I'll advise you to hire private security if you want to patrol the property. Not much else I can tell you." Chief shook her head. Despite the security already in place, Jamie's home was not totally safe from individuals motivated by greed. Or worse.

"Now, I have a few things to tell you." Jamie launched into her news. "First, I told Boo about my work. She didn't recognize me in any of the movies I showed her, although she remembered a couple of the animated films. Said she had seen them with her nephew. Second, if there is a picture, it will just speed up our plan. The family will attend the gallery opening Thursday night in town. Boo will join us and we are inviting the press to cover the event. Boo will be included in pictures with the family, which will be posted. We're hoping someone will see the picture and get in touch. What do you think?"

"Sounds like a plan to me," Chief said. "The paparazzi are starting to descend, so the sooner the better. Gabriela, will you be staying for the opening?"

"No, unfortunately not. I have a flight back to the city Thursday morning. I have a deadline and need to finish the project this week."

"Would I be able to see you sometime tomorrow?" Chief cocked an eyebrow and suppressed a grin as she asked.

"You can start by seeing me tonight for dinner at Sarah's. And, please join us for a family picnic tomorrow." Gabriela did not trust herself to spend time alone with Chief. She did not want to raise Chief's expectations that their casual tryst could become a full-blown love affair.

"Sounds lovely. I'd be honored." Chief nodded her understanding of the invitations as she departed to return to the station to fill out the booking paperwork on Pops.

Gabriela and Jamie spent the rest of the morning by the pool talking, with Max joining them on and off between his other pursuits of happiness. Boo also came and went, balancing respect for Jamie's friendship with Gabriela and wanting to become better acquainted with Jamie's best friend.

Later in the afternoon, as Gabriela played with Max in the pool, Jamie took advantage of time alone with Boo in the kitchen. She relayed Chief's story about the paparazzi with a minimum of emotion, trying to not upset Boo.

"I'm really sorry this happened," Boo responded to the news. "If I weren't here, would he have been sneaking around?"

"Boo, it's what they do. It doesn't matter if you're here or not."

"Do you think he took a picture of us, together, this morning?"

"Yes, I think he did. For me, it doesn't really matter. It's a part of my life. I touch someone in public, it's online in a matter of seconds."

"But this wasn't in public. It would look like just a hug between friends, right?" Boo's expression indicated that she was trying to avoid the truth about the moment in question.

"I have a plan for a little distraction—it's called Fred. No one can resist a great dog story." Jamie grabbed her cell phone to call Dani's number. "Dani, it's Jamie Jordan. How would you like to come out to the office and take a few pictures of Fred? Plus, I have a tip for you about the Crestwood Gallery opening Thursday night." Jamie winked at Boo. She counted on Dani not being able to resist the invitation and she trusted Dani to follow some basic rules in exchange for the exclusive.

"Is four-thirty okay?...Good. Fred and I will see you at the office then."

• • • •

AT EXACTLY FOUR-THIRTY, Jamie and Fred arrived to greet the waiting reporter. Dani took pictures inside the office of Fred staring at her fan mail on the computer screen. Jamie then offered to take Dani to the cliff where the girls were found.

"Is there a catch?" Dani's voice was respectful but suspicious given how assiduously Jamie guarded her privacy.

"Yes and no. No pictures until we get to the spot. If you see anyone along the way, you don't mention it. I have a couple of friends staying with me and I want to respect their privacy."

"I won't play dumb. There are rumors the person who saved Max is staying with you and that's who really found Gee." Dani preferred to put all the cards on the table.

"I don't mean to treat you...I know you're not dumb. Quite the opposite. And you have always been extremely kind to me and my family. I hope you realize how much I appreciate that." Jamie led the way down the path toward the creek. "You should check the morning report at the Sheriff's office. They caught a paparazzi guy out at the lake this morning. We think he took pictures of...my friend. He's in jail right now for assaulting Chief. Mostly likely he will not have the chance to sell anything."

"I heard something from one of the other reporters right before I left the office. I didn't know it had anything to do with you."

"Can we go off the record please?"

"Yes, I will respect that."

"Good. I have heard there is some gossip in town about a mystery person staying with me. The paparazzi are starting to sniff around. I need to put an end to this. The family will be attending the gallery opening for the new local art show."

"Sure, I know about the opening."

"The friend of the family who is staying here with me will be attending with us. We have invited a couple of reporters from Fairfield with the usual press release. I would like for you to come, take pictures of the family, including my friend, and post them. That's all."

"Okay, but this doesn't sound like much of an exclusive. What's the deal?" Dani was intrigued.

Arriving at the rock where the girls were found, Dani took a short video of Fred running along the trail. Fred barked as she hit her mark on top of the cliff. Dani snapped additional pictures of Fred, head held proudly high in the air. It would make the perfect feel-good story.

"Do you know what they call her, my houseguest?" Jamie asked Dani as they began their hike back to the office.

"Boo Charming is the name I hear."

"Yes, that's the deal. We don't know her real name. She can't remember it. She lost her memory when she hit her head saving Max. We need to figure out who she is and locate her family. We hope someone will see her picture and contact us. We don't want to make it known she has amnesia because that would bring the crazies out. I hope you can respect this. If you will please label her a friend of the family and not mention she can't remember her name, I would really appreciate it."

Dani thought for a brief moment about whether complying with the request would compromise her journalistic integrity. She had a wife and young child, and would want someone to be similarly kind to her family, if, goddess-forbid, anything ever happened to one of them.

"Deal. I hope it works. And, maybe, after you find out her name, you can put a word in for me for an exclusive?"

"Deal."

The remainder of the walk to Dani's car was filled with small town gossip and friendly chatter.

Chapter Seventeen

DESPITE THE RECENT drama, dinner at Sarah and Bryan's was a relaxed family gathering. Sarah gave in and allowed Gee to send Dani a picture of her broken ankle in the pneumatic boot to include with the story about Fred. Gee added a statement expressing her remorse for causing trouble and cautioned other children to not make her mistake. *Always tell your parents where you are going. It might not be such a great idea.* There was hope that the public service announcement would persuade Sarah to lessen Gee's sentence from lifetime grounding to twenty years with the chance of parole. Gee also made a great show of apologizing to and thanking Boo, complete with a decorated cake featuring a tall woman standing next to a big black dog.

It did not take long for Dani's story about Fred to be reposted tens of thousands of times. Oblivious to her fame, Fred lay outside on the porch as if nothing concerned her. As dinner ended, the adults took turns reading out loud online comments about Fred's adventure. They ignored the trolling posts of people accusing the family of animal and child abuse, focusing instead on the laudatory and cute.

Gabriela could barely keep her eyes off of Chief during dinner, though she repeatedly reminded herself this was Jamie's world and she was just visiting. She liked her life in the city with its the faster pace and the buzz of millions of people. But that did not stop her from lusting after another hookup with Chief.

Lessa and Philip told the family about their recent work at the shelter house and a new initiative to provide bicycles to children who otherwise would not have access. They wanted to plan a summer party and hoped a couple of bicycle shops from Fairfield would help fix up donated bikes for the kids. Everyone volunteered to help with the cause, including Boo, who, in the excitement, failed to remember she might not be around much longer.

Boo consulted with Shon about clothes for the gallery opening. The two decided on a sporty look, casual but neat. A lightweight ensemble would be consistent with the summer weather and relaxed tone of the opening. Shon was planning their own outfit, too, but declined to give any hints.

Jamie sat back in her chair, watching the gathering of all the people she loved. Even though the invasion of her privacy earlier that day had left her shaken, at this moment a feeling of contentment settled over her. Jamie hated to call an end to the evening, but it was Max's bedtime.

Max was treated to three bedtime stories—one each from Gabriela, Boo, and Jamie. For Max, it was a trifecta of sweet dreams.

Boo retired to her room shortly after completing her bedtime story duty, while Gabriela joined Jamie in her bedroom to process the events of the day.

"That was a fun evening. I'm glad you're here. Will you be spending more time with Chief?" Jamie was as curious as she was concerned.

"Maybe...no...well, maybe." Gabriela was more certain about what she wanted than how she felt. She deflected by lobbing a question back at Jamie, "What are you going to do about Boo?"

"We must find this María Garcia and find out if they are still married. We need to find out Boo's real name, where she's from, her job. She has a life somewhere." Jamie pondered for a long time before continuing, "I just don't know how or if I'll fit."

Gabriela slipped her arm around her friend and pulled her close.

"Be careful with your heart."

"It might be too late for that." Jamie laid her head on Gabriela's shoulder and closed her eyes.

· · · ·

THE FOLLOWING MORNING, Boo woke early. Wandering into the kitchen, she was surprised to not find Jamie making breakfast. Looking out the window, she spotted Jamie sitting on the patio, alone in her thoughts. Boo made two cups of tea.

"Would you prefer to be alone?" Boo inquired as she offered Jamie a cup.

"Please join me. There's something I want to talk about." Jamie waited for Boo to settle into the chair next to her. "Tomorrow evening, I don't want to give any impression that you and I are...together. If you have a wife, I don't want to do anything to disrespect or jeopardize your relationship. So, if I stand a little farther away than usual, it's because the press will be there taking pictures. I'm sorry."

"Why are you apologizing? The plan is for me to be in a picture, right? Hopefully this will help me find my family. We have to assume that María will be understanding, given the circumstances."

"Good. The other thing is someone from the press might ask you for your name. When I talked to Dani, I asked her not to, but the others might. My suggestion is to say you are a friend of the family here for vacation. If you smile and walk away, they should leave you alone. Shon will keep an eye out and rescue you if you're cornered. They are particularly good at running interference."

"I'm sure it will all be fine. Although seeing Shon in action could be a real treat."

"There was one time at a theater," Jamie reminisced, "when a couple of stalker-fans followed me into the restroom. Shon saw them and came in right behind. When those women saw Shon standing there, all six-feet of their wonderful self, they screamed, *you're in the women's restroom.* Shon just glared at them and said in their deepest voice, *everyone's gotta pee somewhere.* They were not enlightened enough to see the humor and fled. I appreciate my fans, but this was hysterical. I wish I had it on video." Jamie was deeply appreciative of how fierce her loyal assistant could be.

Boo and Jamie leaned back in their chairs, settling into silence until Jamie heard Gabriela making noise in the kitchen.

"Shall we join her?" Jamie asked.

"Jamie, thank you for sharing all of this with me. For making me part of your family." Boo stopped for a moment to look into Jamie's eyes. "I don't know what's about to happen, but this, I will never forget." Boo took Jamie's hand, lifting it to her lips. They both closed their eyes to savor the moment.

• • • •

CHIEF JOINED THE FAMILY for a picnic at the lake around noon. While the kids played in the water, Chief updated Jamie on the detained paparazzi.

"Pops was released on bail this morning. He promised to appear in court next week for a preliminary hearing, but most likely he'll waive it to the Grand Jury so he doesn't have to come back. We're keeping his camera and phone as evidence until the hearing. My hope is we will never see him again."

"Shon told me this morning they have not seen any new pictures online. I guess we'll find out if Pops has anything after he leaves town. Hopefully he'll just write this one off."

Chief left Jamie to wander out to the end of the fishing pier and join Boo.

"Chief, mind if I ask you something?" Boo stared off into the lake.

"Go right ahead."

"Did you and Jamie ever date?"

"Oh gosh no. That would be like dating your sister. We've been friends since high school. Besides, she's not my type."

"Gabriela is your type?"

"Gabriela might be my type, but I'm pretty sure that's not going anywhere. She has her life in the city and I have mine here. I believe they call it star-crossed lovers." Chief sighed.

"Star-crossed lovers...sounds sad. I just can't help but wonder why no one seems to be looking for me, especially if I'm married. What do you think I've done that no one wants to find me?"

"People may be looking for you. They may just not be looking in the right place yet. You're a good person, Boo. We'll find your family, soon."

"How do you know I'm good?"

"I've been at this job for a while now. I like to think I can sense things from watching people. I see how you are with Max and with Jamie. You treat everyone with kindness, even though, given your situation, other people would probably just wallow in self-pity or something worse."

"Thanks, Chief." Boo looked over at Jamie talking with Sarah and Gabriela. "Do you think there would ever be a chance, if someone like me asked out someone like Jamie..."

"Well, I don't think it would offend someone exactly like her if someone exactly like you asked her out." Chief laughed at the innocent transparency of Boo's question, but added, "If that someone was not married, of course."

Embarrassment flushed across Boo's face.

"I really need to find out who I am. Soon."

"And one more thing, while we're talking," Chief leveled her eyes on Boo, "if you ever do anything to hurt Jamie—"

"I'm quite certain they'll never find my body," Boo finished Chief's thought with appropriate finality.

"Exactly." Chief turned back to her fishing pole.

As the water lapped against sand and pebbles at the shoreside, Gabriela, Sarah, and Jamie sat at a picnic table watching the kids play.

"What will you do when Boo leaves?"

Gabriela asked the question, but it was Sarah who closely watched her sister's face.

"I will be grateful for my family and friends. Spend time with Max. He's growing up fast. Get back to work. Make a movie. Miss her." The final thought was the truest.

"Don't," Sarah reached for her sister's hand. "We will find a way to keep Boo in the family. She can't just disappear. Finders keepers." Sarah turned her attention to Gabriela, "When are you going to settle down?"

"Probably never. I don't think I'm the settling type." Gabriela glanced over at Chief. "Although occasionally there is someone who makes me question that."

• • • •

THE REST OF THE DAY was a blur of activity. Shon came to the house with a pile of clothes for Boo to try on. It took five different ensembles before Jamie and Gabriela finally gave their approval to a short sleeve, dusty dark purple button down shirt over lightly faded blue jeans. A black tie and black ankle boots would complete the outfit. Shon evened up Boo's hair with clippers.

"Oh my, you are looking quite fine," Shon admired their handiwork.

The finished product was not lost on Jamie or Gabriela either, who both nodded in agreement.

After dinner and a walk in the cool evening air, everyone turned in for bed early. Tomorrow would be a busy day, concluding with Boo's big debut.

• • • •

THURSDAY MORNING, CHIEF picked up Gabriela after breakfast to drive her to the airport in Fairfield. Max went with Sarah and Marco to soccer practice, leaving Jamie and Boo alone in the house for the first time since early Monday morning.

"Are you ready for this evening?" Jamie asked as they returned to the house from a late morning walk.

"As ready as I can be, I guess. It's what happens after this evening...it's a little scary to think about what my forgotten life might be like. At the same time, I'm scared this won't work."

Jamie reached for Boo's hand, but this time she pulled Boo to her and softly kissed her cheek. When Jamie realized Boo was not pulling away, she kissed the side of Boo's forehead and rubbed her cheek against the side of Boo's soft face. Jamie stopped herself.

"I'm sorry. I...I'm scared too. I'm scared of losing you. I just want to hold onto this moment."

Jamie and Boo looked into each other's eyes. They had each become more certain about how they felt. That was not the unknown.

Boo took a step back, drew a deep breath, and composed herself. She could still feel the moist heat of Jamie's lips on her face. All of her body and soul wanted to lean into a kiss right now.

"I think I'll go take a shower." Boo resisted adding the obvious, *a very cold shower*. This would be a long day of waiting and wondering.

For her part, Jamie resisted the even more obvious reply, *I'll join you*. Instead she headed to the office to take care of various items of business. This would be a very long day indeed.

Chapter Eighteen

JAMIE EMERGED FROM her bedroom dressed for the gallery opening. She wore a modest navy blue, button up shirt with small white polka dots, over white slacks. Jamie's hair was blown dry and swept back from her face. The slightest hint of make-up was a concession to the uneven lighting in galleries and flash photography. Her sandals revealed freshly painted purple toenails matching the color of Boo's shirt.

The understated elegance of Jamie's appearance took Boo's breath away. On seeing the stunning woman standing before her, Boo felt inadequate as an escort for the evening.

"Wow! Are you sure you want to be seen with me?"

"You look absolutely wonderful. I would be seen with you anywhere." Jamie eyes conveyed her appreciation of the woman standing before her and she truly meant the compliment and statement.

Max bounded out of his room in his usual summer shorts and T-shirt. Jamie's family had donated money for a room at the library to be staffed for childcare during the gallery opening. Max's night out would be more casual.

Shon showed up in a bright fuschia jacket over a sapphire blue shirt and aquamarine pants with white deck shoes. Their freshly scrubbed and beaming face completed the ensemble, and attitude.

"I think you just stole my thunder," Boo teased her would-be sibling.

· · · ·

BOO'S NERVOUS ENERGY calmed as the family gathered outside the gallery's side door. The Jordan family entered the gallery as a group but immediately dispersed to greet friends and admire the art. Boo looked at the people already milling around the space, recognizing a few as staff from the hospital. Patient privacy rules prevented them from acknowledging Boo until she approached them. When she did finally make her way close enough to say hello, she received a warm welcome as if she were a long-lost friend.

Dani spotted the Jordan family as they arrived. Everyone was familiar except the tall handsome woman walking beside Shon. Finally, the elusive Boo Charming had emerged. Dani greeted the family and asked for a brief statement, giving Jamie the opportunity to talk about the importance of supporting the arts in every community. Dani then approached Philip, asking questions about the new Bikes-for-Kids program. Finally, Dani made her way toward Boo and Shon.

Shon stepped aside but remained within earshot.

"Hi, I'm Dani Bern from the newspaper. Are you enjoying the show?"

"Yes, very much. There are many talented artists in this area. It's a local treasure." Boo flashed her dimpled smile at Dani with surprising warmth.

Dani sensed Boo's easy going charm and instantly understood the stranger's nickname. Looking from handsome Boo to eye-catching Shon, Dani liked the contrast in style.

"Would you two mind if I took a picture of you together?"

"How about if I assemble the whole family for a group picture?" Shon countered. A picture of just them and Boo would not be the big attention grabber Jamie wanted. Although, their outfit certainly might compensate for the lack of celebrity.

"Great. Shall we take a picture against the back wall, behind the reception table?" Dani suggested. "There's better lighting back there."

Shon nodded, leaving to gather the family and other press. Dani pointed the way for Boo.

"Are you enjoying your visit with the Jordan family?" Dani inquired.

"Yes, I am. It's a beautiful area. Lots of different species of birds nesting this time of year. Wonderful diversity of plants. It seems like there has been an attempt to preserve some of the wetlands around here. It is an amazing eco-system." Boo stopped herself, realizing she was talking to cover her nervousness. "Of course, I'm sure you already appreciate all of that about your hometown."

"I try to appreciate it. You sound like a botanist or ecologist?" Dani asked.

"An ecologist?" A sudden memory seized Boo. "Yes, I am."

The Jordan family walking into the reception area interrupted the memory triggering exchange. Boo and Shon stood between Lessa and Philip with Sarah and Bryan on the other side of Jamie, who was front and center. Everyone smiled as Dani and a photographer from a Fairfield newspaper, as well as several local people, snapped pictures.

A television camera crew from a Fairfield station arrived and began filming. It was a slow news day, making it likely that footage of the event would fill out the late night and early morning shows. Naturally comfortable in front of a camera, Jamie provided a brief statement for the television crew. As the reporters packed up to leave, Jamie looked for Boo, finding her lost in thought, staring at a painting of a butterfly on yellow coneflowers.

"Echinacea paradoxa. I'm an ecologist. Dani said it and I remembered. I work on ecosystem restoration. It's why I know all of the plant names. It's not just a hobby."

"That's great. One more piece of the puzzle. This will make it easier to find out your name. I'll text Chief." Jamie was stunned but not surprised by the sudden memory. Forgetting about the photographers in the room, Jamie reached for Boo's hand, intertwining their fingers as they stood close together admiring the painting.

Seeing the couple holding hands, Sarah and Shon exchanged a look. Linking hands, the two walked up behind Jamie and Boo, hoping the mimicking gesture would diffuse any speculation about Jamie and Boo's relationship.

"Boo remembers she's an ecologist," Jamie reported as she turned her head toward Sarah and Shon. Seeing her sister and assistant holding hands caused Jamie to bite her lip to stifle a hearty laugh, until she realized she was holding Boo's hand. Instead of dropping Boo's hand, Jamie grabbed Sarah's free hand. Now Jamie and Boo looked more like part of a prayer circle than a new couple on a date.

"An ecologist? Great. We need one of those in the family. Now, Shon, if you could just find yourself a plumber and an electrician, we'd really be set." Sarah drew chuckles from the others with her inclusiveness. "What? I know about polyamory. I want Shon to be happy."

The Jordan family stayed at the gallery for well over an hour, visiting with each artist whose work was represented in the show.

Later that evening, Dani posted a group picture online identifying Boo in the caption as a *friend of Jamie Jordan and her family*. The television station in Fairfield used video footage to highlight Jamie's presence at the gallery. Boo appeared in the background, unidentified.

The image receiving the most re-posts overnight was one of Jamie and Boo holding hands in front of a painting, looking at each other. Although the picture was taken from behind, the affection on their faces as they gazed at each other was obvious even with the limited view. Another image, taken after Sarah and Shon joined the circle, showed Boo's full face. The post was titled *Does Jamie Jordan have a new girlfriend?*

· · · ·

THE FOLLOWING MORNING, Jamie read a text from Shon informing her their scheme had worked, maybe just not according to plan. Jamie pulled up the pictures on her phone. There was no denying the look she and Boo shared.

I sure hope María Garcia is not the jealous type, Shon's text read.

Keep an eye on the comments and see what comes up. If someone tries to contact us about Boo, pass it along, no matter how crazy, Jamie texted back.

Boo and Max returned to the kitchen after their morning walk in the woods with Fred.

"Is our plan working?" Boo asked while fixing a snack for Max.

Jamie showed Boo the pictures posted online.

"Nice picture. You look stunningly beautiful, as always." Boo was in an anticipatory good mood and failed to read the photo's caption.

"The pictures are being re-posted because they think you're my new girlfriend," Jamie clarified.

"I have good taste, huh, Max?" Boo winked at the boy, still not grasping the implications.

"Mommy's got a girlfriend, Mommy's got a girlfriend," Max sing-songed his approval.

"Okay, you two, I think you're missing the point. We don't want anyone, like María, to think you are cheating on her?" Jamie was worried about the consequences of the photos for Boo, not herself.

Boo reflected for a moment while placing a bowl of fresh fruit and yogurt in front of Max.

"Sorry. You're right. That was not the intention. But, at least it's getting a lot of attention, and lots of people will see it, right? I thought that was the point? Plus, I'm sure María will understand. We're holding hands, not kissing."

Max heard only the last word and picked up his song, "Mommy and Boo, kissing in a tree—"

"Max, eat your snack, please." Jamie gave Max a firm but kind look. She didn't want Max to think she was angry with him, or there would be anything wrong with her and Boo kissing. Jamie blushed as she looked back at Boo. "I do not know where he learned that song."

The mention of kissing did nothing to quell the longing of either Boo or Jamie to do exactly that. The memory of their near kiss was enough to make both of them look away, but the heat generated by their thoughts was nearly combustible. The rest of the morning featured both of them pacing through the house more than usual as they waited to see what would happen next.

Shon called Jamie mid-afternoon.

"I think we've got something. A María Garcia just commented on a post of the picture of you two holding hands in the gallery. I sent you the link. It says, *Glad you are having a good time. See you next week.* Then a heart. I checked—it's definitely not María Garcia the director. You are not scheduled to be anywhere next week, so it makes sense that she's talking to Boo. It's a woman from upstate New York. I'm trying to find more info now."

"Any profile?"

"It's not public. Do you want me to reply to the comment?"

"Not yet. Let me check with Boo." Jamie took in the news with a mixture of excitement, determination, and sadness. She wanted the plan to work but was not prepared for her feelings when it seemed like it really had. It suddenly felt as if she was about to lose Boo, maybe forever. Jamie shook off her conflicted feelings to locate Boo, who was finishing washing lunchtime dishes.

"Great news. We think we have a lead on María." Jamie showed Boo the post.

"New York. I don't think that's where María and I were married or live. Can we find more information? A picture?"

"Shon's looking now. Their online stalking abilities are considerable, so we should have more info soon. You're welcome to look on the computer if you want?"

"We met...we were both...we worked in a lab together." Boo processed her new memories out loud, "We married in Boston I think. I'm from Colorado, she's from Mexico. Why can't I remember my name when I can remember all of this?"

Seeing Boo's frustration, Jamie pulled Boo into her arms. She wanted to protect Boo from pain, help her find her name and her life. She also wanted to be a part of Boo's future.

Boo relaxed into Jamie's embrace. Max entered in the room and joined them without a word. Boo picked up Max, who put his arms around Jamie and Boo's necks. There was no time for self-pity when a four-year-old offered comfort.

This was the family Boo wanted. It was a feeling she did not remember having before. She needed to find María and remember the kind of relationship they had, if it was anything close to what she was experiencing with Jamie and Max.

Jamie's phone rang, breaking up the family embrace.

"I've narrowed it down," Shon reported. "Do you mind if I come up to the house and show you our leading suspects?"

"Please do. I'll call Chief. We'll need her advice."

Shon arrived five minutes later with their laptop in hand, which they projected on the TV for everyone to follow along the search process. Shon integrated Boo's latest memories, producing new search results.

Looking for distractions from thinking about Gabriela, Chief was more than happy to make the trip out to Jamie's house. Besides, if she was not getting her happy ending she thought someone should. She hoped it would be Jamie.

"Using the information we have—Boo is an ecologist, from Colorado, and María Garcia is from Mexico, lives in New York, and has a brother named Miguel. They were married in Massachusetts, we'll assume they are close in age, they possibly worked in the same place, etcetera...I have it narrowed down to less than a dozen strong possibilities. I can pull up pictures for about half of those." Shon opened several webpages on the screen. "Boo, if you see anyone or anything that looks familiar, just say."

Boo studied the photographs of the women on the screen carefully but did not recognize any of them. Reading the information, she recognized an address. "That one looks familiar."

Shon searched for the address.

"Bingo! A María Garcia lives there. Forty years old. Known relatives include a Miguel Garcia who lives in Dallas. She is a professional, but does not list occupation. Also says she supports marriage equality and reproductive rights."

Jamie and Boo looked to Chief for input.

"If we think that's our María, I have a friend who works that area for the feds. I will ask her to check it out. If it's our gal, we can fill her in, find out Boo's real name, and go from there. Plan?"

"Sounds good." Boo felt relief to finally make progress toward resolution.

• • • •

POPS SAW THE PICTURE of Jamie Jordan holding the hand of the same mystery woman he had taken a picture of her with in a far more intimate pose.

"Shit." Pops' chance at big bucks, along with his camera and phone, were lost. There was one picture, uploaded from his cell phone to cloud storage before the phone drowned in the lake, but it was too grainy and the two people were not identifiable. "Shit."

Retaining a local lawyer in Crestwood wasn't easy since most of the attorneys in the area had some connection to the Jordan family and turned down Pops' business. The attorney who finally agreed to take his defense talked with the prosecutor. The basic deal was, if Pops agreed to never come back to Crestwood, did not claim his camera or phone from evidence, and if no pictures of Jamie were posted, then the charges against him would not be pursued.

Pops pulled up a domain name registration website and typed *Popsweddingphotos.com* in the search box. He pressed the submit button. *Popsweddingphotos.com is not available.*

"Shit."

Chapter Nineteen

CHIEF CONTACTED HER work-friend in New York, a federal officer named Erin O'Donnell. Having met at a professional meeting several years prior, they hit it off and made it a point to hang out together with other female officers during conferences. Chief filled Erin in on the details of the case.

"Would you be able to check out the address I texted and find out if this is the woman we're looking for?" Chief requested. "If it is, give her my number, I'll take it from there and arrange for her to contact Boo."

"I'll check it out this evening. Take me about an hour to drive over there. If she works, she's more likely to be around in the evening." Erin was efficient and intrigued by the story. Unlike most of her work cases, this one might actually have a happy ending.

"I appreciate it. Let me know what you find out." Chief ended the call and turned her attention to Jamie and Boo, who both looked pensive. "I'll call you when I hear something. We should have an answer soon if this is our María."

"Would you care to join us for dinner?" Jamie asked as she returned to stirring the simmering vegetables.

"Thanks, but I need to finish up some paperwork. I've been taking some extra time off lately," Chief sighed.

Jamie and Boo finished preparing dinner, with plenty of help from Max. They talked about the summer weather, Gee learning to use her crutches, and Lessa and Philip's new Bikes-for-Kids project. They exhausted several topics except for the one on their minds the most.

· · · ·

ERIN INFORMED HER WIFE she needed to check something out and would be home before dark. She looked again at the picture of Jamie Jordan holding hands with an unidentified tall, striking looking woman. They looked like girlfriends to Erin. Hopefully María Garcia wouldn't see it that way. Since this was not classified business, Erin would tell her wife the whole story later.

Forty-five minutes later, Erin parked her car in front of the address provided by Chief. She surveyed the street as she walked to the front door. Erin knocked, then listened. No sound. She knocked again, louder this time. Erin did not want to announce to the neighbors she was a federal officer, so she stepped back from the door. No car was obviously associated with this house. However, a lot of people in the neighborhood probably biked, used public transportation, or parked on the street wherever they found a space. She resisted looking in the front windows for fear someone might call the police. She did not want to explain the story to a local officer.

As Erin descended the stoop, a neighbor popped her head out of the house next door. The older woman, wearing an apron, looked Erin over twice before she spoke.

"You lookin' for someone?"

"Yes, I am looking for María Garcia. She live here?" Erin nodded toward the door she had just knocked on.

"What you lookin' for?"

"Nothing bad." Erin put her hands on her hips, intentionally exposing the badge clipped to her belt. "Just need to talk to her. Is she around?"

"She left about an hour ago. Want me to give her a message?"

Erin debated the offer. Clearly this woman was the unofficial neighborhood watch on this block. If Erin left a note on the door, it might blow away or someone might swipe it. Mail came to a street box, not a door slot. Despite the desire to help out Chief, Erin did not want to make repeated trips to chase down María Garcia.

"Yes, thank you, that would be helpful." Erin took a pen and paper from her pocket to write a short note, *María Garcia, Please give me a call. I would like to talk to you about your spouse.* Erin added her name and phone number.

The message was cryptic, but would have to suffice. Since Boo's real name was unknown, there was no use using a new nickname María would be unfamiliar with. It was highly likely the nosy neighbor would tell María about Erin's badge, giving the request credibility and some urgency. Erin folded the piece of paper and handed it to the woman.

"I'll give it to her as soon as she gets home." The older woman made no pretense of not reading the note. "I saw her leave with her wife about an hour ago. Do you want me to keep this a secret from Isabella?"

Erin was taken aback by the news that her target was married to someone who most definitely was not missing. Erin adjusted her thought process. Either this was not the woman Chief was looking for, or maybe this was Boo's ex-wife from a forgotten divorce.

"Right, I should have written ex-spouse." Erin retrieved the note and wrote in *ex-* above spouse, hoping that would suffice.

"I'll give it to her." The older woman frowned as she took the note back. She shut the door as Erin descended the steps, and watched suspiciously from her front window as Erin walked back to her car.

On the drive home, Erin called Chief to report.

"Unless Boo has forgotten her divorce, this may be a dead-end."

Chief thanked Erin and promised her a nice dinner at their next conference as payment for the trouble. All they could do now was wait and see if this María Garcia had a missing ex-spouse and would be intrigued enough by the note to contact Erin.

An hour after Erin departed, María and Isabella arrived home from Friday evening dinner and shopping for groceries. They parked in the first available spot and each grabbed bags to carry in. Isabella unlocked the front door while María finished collecting bags and locking the car. As María ascended the steps to the house, the neighbor woman's head popped out of her doorway.

"María, honey, would you help me with something when you have a minute?" the older woman called out.

"Sure, let me put these groceries in the house. I'll be over in a few minutes, Miss Miriam." It was not unusual for María's neighbor to ask for her help with a minor task she could probably do herself but really just wanted company. Plus, Miss Miriam often had some tidbit of amusing neighborhood gossip.

"Would you mind if I run next door and see what Miss Miriam wants?" María asked as she set the groceries on the kitchen counter.

"No, go ahead. I'll put these away." Isabella blew María a kiss.

María hopped down the steps and hurried to her neighbor's front door.

"What can I help you with tonight, Miss Miriam?"

"I thought you should know someone was lookin' for you about an hour ago. Her name was Erin O'Donnell, a cop. Didn't say she was a cop but made sure I saw the badge. Nice looking. About your age, honey. Red hair. I'll bet she's Irish. Drove a black car."

"Did she say what she wanted to talk to me about?"

"She asked me to give you a note, but when I said something about your wife, Isabella, she took the note back and added the part about the ex right here." Miss Miriam produced the note and pointed to the addition of *ex-* above *spouse*. "She acted real strange about it."

"Thanks." María was not surprised by Miss Miriam reading the note but had no intention of discussing her marital status with the neighbor. "Now, what do you need my help with?"

"I just promised I would give this to you the minute you came home. You go on now." It was clear to Miss Miriam that María would not be offering any information about the note or the visit by a cop.

María returned home, shaking her head as she walked into the kitchen where Isabella had settled with a cup of tea.

"We have a problem," María declared as she showed Isabella the note and repeated what Miss Miriam had said.

They grabbed a computer tablet, quickly finding Erin O'Donnell's name listed as an employee of a federal law enforcement agency. Apprehension gripped them both.

"What are we going to do? Why are they looking for Jirafa?" Isabella was near tears.

"I have no idea. Now the feds think you and I are married. That does not look good at all. We need to sign these papers and file them as soon as possible. And, I need to warn Jirafa the feds were here. I don't want her in trouble. We did not do anything wrong, but I don't want to talk to anyone until she and I are on the same page."

"Where is she?"

"She's out on a job. Not due back until next week. I've called her a couple of times and texted her, but no response. I assumed she was off the grid, but then I saw a picture of her online. I'm positive it's her. She was with Jamie Jordan, the actor, at an art gallery. I'll find it." María searched for the picture to show Isabella. "It's definitely her, right?"

"If it's not, then she has an identical twin. A much better dressed twin. That's definitely her dimple. Hair's shorter than the last time I saw her, but that's not unusual for her. What's she doing holding hands with Jamie Jordan at an art show?"

"Right? I don't know, but she finds herself in some pretty interesting situations with her job. Anyway, I need to talk to her before anything else happens."

María spent the next hour making phone calls and sending texts to mutual friends and Jirafa's work colleagues. Finally, a colleague texted back explaining he dropped Jirafa at a diner just north of Crestwood three weeks prior. The plan was for her to meet up with a ride to a remote field study site. He heard no more so he figured she made it and was out of touch for a while. Unfortunately, he could not remember the name of the person picking her up.

"What do you think I should do?" María asked Isabella.

"This gallery is in Crestwood. Why would she still be there?"

"Why doesn't she answer her phone or texts? None of it makes sense. And now the feds seem to be looking for her, through me." María found a map of Crestwood on her phone app. "Depending on traffic and construction, it's about a day's drive."

"Do you want to try to find her? I don't think I can take off from work." Isabella implicitly gave María permission to conduct a search for Jirafa.

"I'll start out early in the morning." María took Isabella's hands in hers and kissed Isabella softly on the lips. "Thanks, babe, I appreciate your support. We need to clear this up."

"It's my future, too. Plus, now we'll worry about her until we find out what the heck is going on."

Isabella grabbed a suitcase from the hall closet and followed María upstairs. The cats sniffed the bag as the couple made quick work of packing clothes and essentials. María looked with deep affection at her partner of nearly two years. They had moved to their new home two months prior and María looked forward to starting a family with this beautiful, gentle woman. There was just one small detail to take care of first—finalizing her divorce from Jirafa.

Jirafa was part of the package deal when Isabella met María. While liking your partner's wife might seem strange to other people, in this case it was the way to María's heart. Besides, Isabella enjoyed Jirafa's company, and Jirafa had been nothing but kind, thoughtful, and generous to her.

María pulled Isabella into her arms, instigating a long, slow kiss. There was no urgency, but there was an intention.

"Mi alma...mmmm." María nuzzled Isabella's neck as she lay her partner gently onto the bed. "I'll finish packing later."

. . . .

CHIEF CALLED JAMIE late in the evening. With Max was already in bed, Jamie put Chief on speaker phone.

"Erin says this María Garcia is married, apparently not to Boo. If you are divorced, Boo, this may still be her. Otherwise, it's not our gal. Hopefully she'll call Erin either way. In the meantime, we'll follow up tomorrow on some of Shon's other leads. I'm sorry I don't have better news."

"Thanks, Chief. I really appreciate you trying." Boo's shoulders sank and her head drooped.

"Thanks, Chief. I'll talk to you tomorrow." Jamie ended the call and moved closer to Boo on the sofa. "Are you okay?"

"Yes, I'm sure we'll find her. I'm just confused. The address sounded familiar." Tears of frustration filled Boo's eyes.

Jamie stroked Boo's head and rubbed her muscled arm until Boo finally gave in and laid her head in Jamie's lap.

"Boo, look at me, please?" Jamie lifted Boo's head until their eyes made contact. "Stay with me tonight."

Boo understood she was being invited into Jamie's bed. She realized this was the only thing Jamie could think of at this point to comfort Boo and make sure she did not feel alone. Resisting the urge to kiss Jamie had become a daily challenge. This invitation presented the ultimate test of her self-restraint.

Seeing the conflict on Boo's face, Jamie addressed the unspoken.

"Boo, I'm not expecting you to have sex with me. I just don't want you to be alone tonight, and, truth be told, I don't want to be alone tonight either. I want to hold you. Please let me?" Jamie expressed her own vulnerability in hopes Boo would stop resisting.

"Okay," was the only word Boo could manage as she stood to follow Jamie.

Once in the bedroom, Jamie disappeared into the bathroom to wash her face and change into pajamas. When she emerged, Boo was lying, fully clothed, on top of the bed covers. Jamie lay down on the bed allowing Boo to snuggle next to her. Placing one arm under Boo's head, Jamie pulled Boo close.

Neither woman was sure how much she would sleep. The closeness provided the comfort each sought, but also kindled the flames of attraction igniting between them.

Chapter Twenty

THE ALARM BUZZED AT four-thirty in the morning, but María was already awake and preparing to leave. Isabella made breakfast and packed a lunch, including several snack bars and homemade cookies. They shared the goodbye kiss lovers share when one must go on an unexpected journey, alone.

"I'll call you. Te amo." María kissed Isabella one more time and began her trip.

"I love you too," Isabella called out as she lingered at the door.

• • • •

JAMIE FELT BOO'S LIPS press against hers. Very softly at first, then with more pressure. Boo's lips were much softer than Jamie had imagined. And she had imagined this kiss many times. The first kiss was a sweet surprise Jamie wanted burned into her memory. It was almost as if Boo's lips and hers were melting together.

Jamie's eyes flew open. The time on the clock was much later than she expected. Boo was still in her arms. An overwhelming urge to wake Boo by kissing her threatened to make the dream into a reality. A deep sigh strengthened Jamie's resolve—stealing a kiss was not an option. It would violate the trust she built with Boo. Plus, it was clear where a kiss would lead—to more kisses. And that would lead to...Jamie was trying to decide if what would follow would be tender love-making or urgent sex when Boo stirred, opening her eyes.

"Good morning," Jamie spoke first, sounding far more casual than her aroused body felt.

"Good morning." Boo blinked a couple of times to clear the sleep from her eyes.

Neither woman wanted to leave their embrace. Both were content to linger in the moment. Max had other plans as he entered his mother's bedroom without knocking.

"Mom," he whined, half asleep, "breakfast." Max crawled into bed, snuggling against Jamie's free side. His eyes soon settled on Boo, causing him to smile sweetly at her.

"Come on, tigre, I'll make us something." Boo reached across Jamie's torso to tousle Max's hair. She then rolled out of bed, gently lifted Max up into her arms, and walked toward the kitchen. Max reached up to run his hand through Boo's hair as she kissed his forehead.

Jamie watched the display of obvious affection between the two. Her heart was lost. She was falling deeper in love as the scenes of perfectly ordinary, yet joyful domesticity played out each day with Boo.

Jamie forced herself out of bed and followed the sounds of breakfast preparations. The morning routine had begun. This ritual would end sooner or later, one way or another, but for now it enveloped them in the comfort of knowing what happens next.

"I need to spend some time in the office today," Jamie jump started the conversation. "I have to start thinking about what my next project will be."

Boo stared into her cereal bowl, uninterested in its contents. It seemed that everyone else's life was moving forward except hers. A feeling of being adrift washed over her.

Picking up on Boo's mood, Jamie devised an impromptu plan for the day.

"Boo, I was wondering if you would do me a big favor? Mom and Dad are headed to Fairfield later this morning for a couple of meetings. Max really likes the children's museum there. How would you feel about taking Max there today? If you're up for it. It can be loud and chaotic."

"Really?" Boo perked up.

"Max, would you like to go to the children's museum in Fairfield today?"

"Yes!"

"I don't think we can disappoint him now." Jamie shrugged innocently. "I'll call Mom and Dad. I really appreciate this. And Max does too. Right, Max?"

"Yes!"

Boo looked at Jamie for a moment. Jamie was obviously doing her a favor, not the other way around. "Are you sure? I mean, what do I do if someone recognizes him as your kid or something happens?"

"Boo—number one, Max doesn't get recognized unless he is with me or someone in the family. Otherwise, he looks just like every other kid. In this case, everyone will assume he's your child or you're a relative. Number two, I trust you. It's very clear you and I feel the same about Max—we'd give our life to protect him. Number three, if you need help, there are a lot of staff at the museum, and Mom and Dad will be a phone call away. I am totally comfortable with this."

Jamie dialed her phone, making arrangements with her parents to pick up Boo and Max in an hour. Jamie would meet them in Crestwood in the late afternoon for dinner. It was the perfect plan. After ending the call, Jamie walked around the kitchen table to kiss Max on the head. Lifting Max's face, she zeroed in on him with stern eyes.

"Max, you need to stay with Boo today. You must not run off for any reason. If you need to go somewhere, you must take Boo with you. I am trusting you to bring Boo back home to me. Do you understand?"

"Yes, Mom, I'll bring Boo home. I promise."

"Okay, now go find some clothes and let me see them before you put them on. And bring me your backpack so we can put some stuff in it." Jamie sent Max off to his room with a pat on his butt.

Boo was amused by the way Jamie handled Max until Jamie turned on her.

Jamie walked around the table and kissed Boo on the head. She lifted Boo's face, eyes zeroed in on her target.

"Boo, you need to stay with Max and you must not run off for any reason. I am trusting both of you to come back home to me. Do you understand?" Jamie wanted to seal the lecture with a kiss on Boo's lips but resisted.

"Yes, ma'am. I promise we will both come home to you."

"Good. I love you both and I need you both here with me at the end of the day." The word *love* escaped Jamie's lips before she could censor herself, but she realized she did not want to take it back. Although the sentiment was safer linked as it was to Max, the feeling was one she wanted to express to Boo.

"We love you, too, and we will not fail in our mission." Boo's mischievous look deepened her dimple. "I will find some clothes. Do you want to see them before I put them on?"

Jamie's internal response was, *I want to see you putting them on and then take them off of you.* Her external response was deadpan.

"I trust you, but please do not mix paisley with plaid. And put a hat on. Apparently that is all you need to disguise yourself."

As Boo passed, Jamie patted her on the butt, too. After Boo left the room, Jamie exhaled, realizing she needed to watch herself more closely. She was acting more and more flirty with someone else's wife. She would not want another woman flirting with Boo if Boo were her wife. And, while Jamie was trying to keep it all in good fun, there was intention behind the words she passed off as joking.

. . . .

MARÍA SPENT PART OF her drive on the phone calling people who Jirafa was likely to be in contact with. No one had heard from her in several weeks but that was typical when Jirafa was out in the field working. Jirafa often traveled to remote locations, plus she would take off on back country hikes for several days at a time. She was not reckless, just out of contact for long stretches of time.

María finally reached someone from the field site where Jirafa was supposed to arrive three weeks prior. Jirafa had not shown up, but no one thought much of it, assuming she had been delayed or was at another job site. The person María talked with did not remember who was scheduled to pick up Jirafa in Crestwood.

"So we know she does not have her truck, she was dropped off in Crest-wood, but we don't know who was supposed to pick her up," María said, filling Isabella in on the day's conversations. "We know she has a job she should be working on, but we don't know why she has not shown up. And we don't know why she seems to still be in Crestwood."

"We do know she's still alive and apparently she's done some clothes shopping." Isabella was always looking on the bright side. "Maybe she met somebody, fell in love, and decided to stay in Crestwood."

"Yeah, right," María couldn't help but adopt a somewhat sarcastic tone, "that would be totally out of character for her to just give up her work. She's not independently wealthy, and I'm not sure there's a woman who could compete with her passion for her work." María had firsthand knowledge of how dedicated Jirafa was to her work, often to the detriment of personal relationships. Even though it was long past, María could still be cautious in her relationship with Isabella because of her experience with Jirafa.

"That's true." Isabella understood María's tone. "I guess when you find her you'll find out what happened. The more important thing is to find her before the feds do, just in case."

"I'm still a couple of hours away. I'll check at the diner where she was dropped off. I guess I could try to contact Jamie Jordan, but I doubt her phone number is listed. And it's not like I can go to the cops and file a missing person report when her picture is posted online. We know where she is, we just don't know why she's out of touch."

"Okay, text me when you get there. Anda con cuidado, mi amor."

• • • •

"COULDN'T SHE HAVE MARRIED someone named Oriwennla Xael-vette Zuriaria?" Shon's search for the elusive María Garcia resulted in an exasperated tone.

"You better search and make sure you're not making fun of someone's real name." Jamie felt a similar, but more aching frustration.

"I can't believe she wasn't the right one. She's the closest match we have. I sent some other possibilities to Chief, but none of them look good enough to follow up on. Do you think Boo just forgot about being divorced?" Shon sat back in their chair to think.

"Anything is possible, but she seems sure she's still married. And the comment online indicated an expectation to see Boo next week, so we assume someone is expecting her to be somewhere. Have there been any more comments?" Jamie asked.

"Not that I have seen but there are tens of thousands of comments. There's no way to read them all. I searched for phrases. Plus, things are re-posted all over. We'll never see most of the things people post."

"Take a break, Shon. We need to be patient. Next week, we will do another appearance."

"It might start to look like you two are really an item." Shon unconvincingly attempted to conceal a grin.

Jamie ignored Shon's comment to avoid denying it. She was busy making a list of issues she wanted to speak with her agent about, and Boo was not on the list. Jamie had submitted a short read on video for one of the meetings she cancelled earlier in the week. Her agent was working on the endorsement deal. Finally, there was a film project she was intrigued by, but she wanted more information about the production team and who would be directing before she expressed interest.

Jamie also needed to talk to her agent about transitioning from acting to more behind the camera work. Jamie's primary goal was to find work she had a passion for, but would keep her out of the direct spotlight. She wanted to spend more time with Max as he grew up, and, possibly, include another child in their family. And, hopefully, add a romantic partner.

As her career progressed, Jamie spent more time on set learning about directing and production. Her most recent directors were happy to explain their scene decisions and talk at length about how to create a guiding vision for a film. Being able to see a whole project, not just her part, was a skill Jamie needed to learn if she wanted to try her hand at directing even a small film. Directing was hard work, but it would be a fresh challenge.

• • • •

BOO AND MAX'S VISIT to the children's museum was a welcome change in routine. A couple of times during the day, Boo sought refuge from the shrillness of excited children's screams, but she never let Max out of her sight. On Max's part, whenever he noticed Boo was not by his side, he searched until he found her. Then, taking her hand, he would lead her back into the raucous fray.

Lessa and Philip successfully negotiated with two bicycle shops to support their Bikes-for-Kids project before retrieving Boo and Max from the museum. On the drive home, Lessa glanced in her rearview mirror at the two sleeping figures in the back seat. Lessa and Philip were growing fonder of Boo as they spent time together and watched her interact with Max and Jamie. They wanted Boo to be happy and hoped to keep her in their lives. This was especially important to them given Jamie's obvious feelings.

Chapter Twenty-one

"THERE'S STILL A CHANCE this is the María we're looking for." On the way to her parent's house for dinner, Jamie had phoned Gabriela, looking for solace. "It's just harder and harder to wait for answers," Jamie's frustration surfaced as she talked to her dear friend.

"Well, if this is the right María, then the good news is she's either a polygamist so she will not care if you and Boo hook up, or Boo forgot they are divorced so you two can hook up."

"I hear a theme in those thoughts, but that's not my priority right now. If Boo forgot they're divorced, given what she said to you in the hospital, she's probably still in love with María." Jamie struggled with her conflicted feelings of wanting Boo to be happy and wanting Boo to be happy *with her*.

"What do you want, Jamie? You want to help Boo find her family, but that's not all that's going on here." Gabriela was incisive, cutting to the chase.

"I want to know if...if Boo is available...I want to ask her out on a date, or something, not just friends."

"You're already living together, don't you think a date would be kinda postmature?" Gabriella lightened the mood by teasing her friend. "Anyway, when was the last time you asked someone on a date?"

"It has been a while. I guess I'll have to ask you for some tips on modern dating protocol," Jamie responded to her friend who was far more active on the dating scene.

"What you really want to find out is if you can kiss her and hook up."

"Yes. I want to kiss her, but only if she is not married and doesn't have a partner."

"Just do it. If you find out she's married, she leaves and it was a momentary indiscretion. If she's not married, then, well, you'll have a head start."

"There have been a couple of times when I thought we were about to kiss, but Boo always backs away. She has integrity. Plus, I really don't want to interfere in someone's marriage or relationship. Who knew integrity could be such a buzzkill." Jamie plaintive tone lead to a resigned sigh. "I'm pulling into Mom and Dad's. I'll update you when we find out something new. Chao."

Max ran to greet his mother as she walked through the front door.

"Mom, we saw a dinosaur today. We went into a cave. And there was a space ship. I flew it. And a real train," Max talked until he was breathless. Having exhausted his report, he pulled her into the kitchen where the rest of the family was making dinner.

"How did it go today?" Jamie inquired as she greeted her father will a kiss on the cheek.

"It went well," Philip reported. "Two bike shops will donate their time to perform the more complicated restoration of the bikes. They'll teach us to do the rest and come provide lessons on basic bicycle maintenance."

"I would call that a success. Please, let me know how I can help." Jamie walked around the kitchen bar to where Boo was making a salad and kissed her on the cheek, too. "You survived."

"We had fun," Boo's eyes twinkled. "Can I go back soon? Please, mom, please?"

Max looked up from his dinosaur coloring book to see what his mother's answer would be.

"If you're good," Jamie winked at Boo in a matching playful spirit.

"Me, too?" Max chimed in.

"You too, Max. Now, put your coloring book away and go wash up for dinner." Jamie turned back to Boo. "Did everything really go okay?"

"I saved three children from a flying Pterodactyl, found two lost kids in the mineral cave, and stopped a runaway locomotive with my bare hands. All in a day's work," Boo deadpanned her heroics. "It was loud, but Max and I took a nap on the drive home thanks to our wonderful chauffeurs."

"Honey," Lessa interrupted Boo and Jamie's debriefing, "Chief will be joining us for dinner. Would you please text her that we are about to sit down?"

Chief arrived a few minutes later and everyone took a seat, passing bowls and plates of food. Max ate and told Chief about his day at the same time until his mother asked him to refrain from spitting food everywhere in his excitement. The conversation took on a quieter tone.

"I'm sorry our lead doesn't seem to have worked out. We'll keep looking." Chief sensed Boo's disappointment and wanted to bring an end to this mystery.

"Thanks for everything you've done. I admit I was really bummed last night, but I feel better today. We'll find María, I'm sure of it. In the meantime, it felt really good to have something to do today. How long will it take for me to legally acquire a new name and whatever else I need for a driver's license? I want to hunt for a job."

"The process could take quite a while. If we had your old name, it would be easier to file a motion for a name change," Lessa explained, "but without having your old name, it will require several motions and court orders for a name, apply for a social security number, and other things to establish a new identity. Basically, the court is interested in finding out if you have any old debts, if you are committing fraud, or trying to avoid something like criminal charges or civil liability. And without your old name, it's harder to establish those conditions."

"What might help is establishing a schedule and finding something meaningful, a purpose for each day." Philip reached for Boo's hand across the table. "If you would like to help me with some volunteer work, I'd love to have you."

"I would really like to volunteer, but I also need a job. I keep borrowing money and have no idea how or when I will pay it back."

"Unfortunately, it will be nearly impossible to find a job without identity documents. With no official identity, an employer cannot pay you except in cash, which quickly becomes a legal gray area," Lessa explained the law, unfair as it could be. "I will help you with the paperwork to start the process. The first task is to choose your new name. Any thoughts?"

The dinner party spent several minutes coming up with suggestions for names. *Boo Charming* was the obvious. Clearly an appropriate nickname, but the group decided it was too glib as a professional or permanent name. Max contributed a couple of suggestions, including *Yeti Jorge Jordan*, after two characters from his favorite books.

"That's a great name. We'll search it and see if it's already taken." Boo was touched Max assumed she would share his last name.

As dinner ended, Max asked if he could stay with his grandparents for the night. Lessa and Philip agreed, always prepared to spend time with their grandson. Chief headed back to the office to check on the evening shift officers. Boo and Jamie lingered a short time before departing for home.

• • • •

MARÍA HAD ARRIVED IN Crestwood late afternoon. Her first stop was the diner on the edge of town. Taking a seat at the counter, she struck up a polite conversation with the middle-aged woman serving her. María was handsome, yet unassumingly so. She was slightly taller than average and inhabited her muscled body with ease. Her straight jet black hair was pulled back, leaving her piercing brown eyes in full view. Her voice was melodic in a way that sounded almost poetic when she spoke, inevitably disarming even the most distrusting with her rapport.

"Where you headed, honey?" the server asked María.

"I have arrived at my destination," María glanced at the woman's name tag, "Juanita. I'm trying to find a friend who's staying in town. She likes good food, so maybe you've seen her." María showed Juanita a picture of Jirafa.

"Someone else was in here looking for your friend. One of the Sheriff's deputies, a couple of weeks ago. I'll tell you what I told him. She ordered breakfast, said she just got to town, then asked me how far the library was. Haven't seen her since, but I think her picture was in the local paper, with Jamie Jordan. Did you see that?"

"Yes, I did. That's what brought me to town. Thought I might catch up with her. Any idea where I should look?"

"Rumor has it she's staying with Jamie. Guess they're friends. What did you say your friend's name is?"

María was not sure how much to divulge, although Jirafa seemed to be hiding in plain sight. "Her friends call her Jirafa—it's a nickname from college."

"Well, she is that. Hope you find her," Juanita said as she moved on to her next customer.

María left a large tip and continued her drive into Crestwood. Downtown was a bucolic place late on a Saturday afternoon in the summer. Several adults with their children were seated on a patio outside the ice cream shop. City Hall was quiet and the library looked nearly empty. Since this was Jirafa's last known destination, María parked and entered the building.

María took advantage of a free library computer to search county property records. She easily turned up an address for Jamie's parents' house in town. Not finding a property under Jamie's name, she located several addresses deeded to limited liability corporations and trusts with ambiguous names. She made a list to drive by and check them out. She could have asked someone where Jamie lived, but she didn't want to look like a celebrity stalker or call too much attention to her presence in town. Asking would be the last resort.

María drove to the edge of downtown, easily finding the house registered to Alessandra and Philip Jordan. The old wood-frame farmhouse with a wide wrap-around porch had a large picture window on the front. There were two cars parked in the garage and a large SUV in the driveway.

María parked her car along the street to call Isabella. With Isabella's assistance, María planned a route to drive-by the properties on her list. Isabella looked at a satellite map as they talked and helped María prioritize the order of most to least likely.

While making notes, María noticed a young white sandy haired man sitting in a car parked a couple of vehicles behind her. Distracted by house numbers while she drove along the street, she had not seen him until now. He was directly across from the Jordan house. The tinted windows on the car were closed, concealing his presence from three sides. But looking back through his front windshield, she saw him clearly. He was watching the Jordan house.

The man lifted a camera and pointed it toward the Jordan house. He rolled down the window just enough for a clear shot. María swiveled her head to the left and saw the SUV from the Jordan driveway backing into the street. She could not see who was in the SUV through its tinted windows, but the man in the car was taking pictures of the occupants.

"What the—?" María tried to decide if this was police surveillance or paparazzi. If it was the police, she did not want to give herself up by confronting the man in the car. If it was paparazzi and Jirafa was in the SUV, she wanted to stop him from taking Jirafa's picture until she could find out more about what was going on.

María did not have long to make up her mind. As soon as the SUV took off in the other direction, the man pulled out and drove past María's car. She followed the car, which had out-of-state, not government plates. More likely than not, this was a paparazzi.

Following the car in the light weekend traffic was easy. The man soon pulled into a local hotel on the highway at the edge of town. María was not planning to stay there, but maybe her plans had just changed.

Parking at the opposite end of the lot, María walked back toward the main office along the sidewalk in front of the room doors. The man from the car she had followed walked toward her from the opposite directing, carrying a camera bag in one hand. As he approached, she spotted the hotel linen room and reached for the door handle. The door opened, revealing a housekeeper seated at a small table, eating her dinner and watching a small TV. María stood in the open doorway as the man passed behind her.

"Bring me a couple of towels. Room one-fifteen," the man ordered without looking at her.

"Don't worry, I'll take care of this." María grabbed towels from a shelf next to the door, winking at the housekeeper.

The house keeper nodded without comment.

"Housekeeping," María announced at room 115.

"It's open," the man called out.

María let herself in. The man was seated at the desk, looking at pictures on the back of his camera.

"Just leave the towels on the bed," he ordered, again without looking up.

María stood behind him, looking over his shoulder.

"Hey, get out." The man started to stand, but María put her hands on his shoulders and shoved him back down into the chair.

"What you got there?" María took possession of the camera with her right hand while simultaneously grabbing his left arm and pinning it behind him. She used her body to push the chair under the desk, trapping him.

"What the—who are you? I'm calling the cops. Fuck—" the man sputtered.

María peered at the picture on the screen. Jirafa was in the front seat of the SUV next to Jamie Jordan. Finding the trash icon on the camera menu, María instructed the camera to delete all of the stored photographs. Then she ejected the memory disk into her hand.

"It's illegal to take pictures of people on private property without their con-sent." María sounded official even though she had no clue if what she said was true.

"Fuck. I heard about you. You're the Sheriff who busted Pops. I'm reporting you."

"And you know what happened to Pops." María did not have a clue what this guy was talking about, but she went with it. "Is that what you want?"

"Fuck you. Somebody will get the picture, sooner or later. You can't be everywhere."

"Well, I'm here now. And I suggest that you not be here anymore. Get out of town before I..." María decided it was best to let the implied threat hang. She took a step back, walked two short steps to the bathroom, flicked the disk in the toilet, and flushed it.

As the man pushed the chair back from the desk to stand up, María shoved him down again. This time she grabbed his cell phone. "Don't get up. I'll let myself out."

María exited the hotel room, tossing the phone in the nearest garbage dumpster. As she drove away, she saw the man muttering to himself, clearly debating whether to dive in to find his phone.

Chapter Twenty-two

ON THE DRIVE HOME AFTER dinner, Boo regaled Jamie with stories of her day. She spared no detail when talking about Max's curiosity and delight in discovery. Boo's mood was considerably brighter and it was clear she had taken immense pleasure in her task of accompanying Max to the museum.

"Thank you. I really appreciate you taking Max. As much as I hate to miss sharing these experiences, I love that you were there with him." It was becoming increasingly difficult for Jamie to imagine her life, or Max's, without Boo in it.

"I appreciate your trust." This time it was Boo who reached for Jamie's hand.

A quick phone call with Shon established they had turned up no new promising leads on María.

"Would you like to watch a movie or something?" Jamie asked as she created room in the fridge for leftover pieces of blueberry pie her mother had insisted she take home for later.

"I think I need something quiet."

"Of course," Jamie said. "Sit on the patio and watch the sunset?"

"Sounds wonderful. Anything I can help you with in here?"

"No, go ahead, I'll join you in a few minutes."

Boo took a seat on the patio, with Fred laid out on the cool flagstones. When Jamie appeared, she had changed into sweatpants and pulled on a long-sleeved shirt against the cool evening breeze. Boo appreciated the casual beauty of the woman lounging next to her.

"Do you think there's someone out there right now taking pictures?" Boo stared at the edge of the woods. "This is a freaky feeling."

"I don't like it either, but I'm past caring." Jamie grinned at Boo with a hint of mischief. "I don't want to disrespect your relationship, but I think it's time we grab María's attention. I just hope she's not the violently jealous type."

"Should we...do something else...for publicity?" Boo cringed. "I can't believe I just said that. I'm sorry."

"No, don't be. I'm thinking it too. How would you feel about doing something with Mom and Dad's Bikes-for-Kids program? We could both volunteer, provide publicity for the program, and put a few more pictures out there?"

"I think it's a great idea. I really admire your parents and their commitment to the community." Boo stared intently at the edge of the wood again before continuing. "Jamie, thank you...for last night. I..." All Boo could think was *I really want to kiss you right now.*

"Anytime," Jamie responded without being flirtatious, "but let's hope this is resolved soon, because I hate to see you sad."

Boo reached across the space between their chairs, enveloping Jamie's hand in her own. She leaned slightly toward Jamie, lifting the soft hand to her lips and gently kissing it. Boo resisted the urge to continue kissing her way up Jamie's arm. The look on Jamie's face was one of invitation and desire. Boo allowed their intertwined hands to dangle between them, looking out at the sun disappearing behind the hills.

With the light fading fast, Jamie finally broke the silence.

"Boo, you are very important to me. I want you in my life and in Max's life. I know it's selfish of me. I want you to find your life, your family and friends. I would like to be a part of that, if you'll let me."

"I want you, and Max, in my life, too. And the rest of your family." Boo struggled to contain her emotions. "I'm sure you have noticed I have become very attached to all of you these past couple of weeks. We'll figure it out."

"Do you want to..." Jamie left open the implied invitation back to her bed.

"Maybe I should just stay here for a while longer." Boo barely dared to glance at Jamie lest she give in and follow Jamie to her bedroom.

Jamie rose from her seat, leaning down to kiss Boo on the cheek. The heat generated by the simple act of affection left them both light headed. Jamie disappeared into the house.

Fred sighed heavily, remaining stretched out at Boo's side.

• • • •

MARÍA DROVE BY THE first couple of houses on her list. When she drove past the gated driveway, she sensed it was the right place. A small house with several parking spaces in front, barely visible from the road, looked as though it could be an office. The satellite image had shown another, larger house with a pool further back the driveway, obscured from view from the road. María continued another half mile down the highway until she found a second gate. Of all the possibilities, this was the most likely to be the Jordan family home.

Turning around and driving past the two driveways again, María reasoned that the one leading to the small office and larger house with pool was more likely to be Jamie's driveway. The satellite had revealed what appeared to be a small lane between the houses. While driving the section of highway, María had noticed a trail cross between the two driveways. There did not appear to be a fence surrounding the property, although one could be farther in the woods, invisible from the highway.

One option was to pull up to the gate and use the callbox to ask for Jirafa. The direct approach might work, but there was still a mystery about why Jirafa did not answer phone calls or texts. Clearly she was not being held against her will. Of course, it was also possible it was just a rumor and Jirafa was not staying with Jamie Jordan. But, given that María had seen the pictures of them together at the art gallery and in the SUV, it seemed more likely than not Jirafa was here. María pulled into the lake parking lot to call Isabella.

"If they are just friends, then Jirafa has probably told her about me. But, if they are dating, then maybe she's not answering the phone because she's not telling this woman everything. That really doesn't sound like Jirafa, but then again none of this does."

"Cariña, Jirafa has been under a lot of stress lately. Her life is changing and people react very differently to stress," Isabella offered an understanding perspective, "but if you're right, if she is dating this woman and hasn't told her, then it might wreck it if you show up uninvited. Do you think it's possible to talk with her alone, before this Jamie person or anyone else sees you?"

"I'd like to find a way. I was thinking about walking in. Jirafa can't sit still. She'll be out for a walk or something."

"What if this woman has security, or they're joined at the hip? Don't get yourself arrested, or worse." Isabella worried more about María's safety at this point than Jirafa's.

"You forget who you're talking to," María retorted with as much pride as bravado.

"That's what worries me. Do not make me come bail you out." Isabella's final directive ended the call.

María returned to town to check into a hotel room. She considered her options. The driveway presented the simple route, but she assumed there were security cameras monitoring every movement along the drive. There might also be cameras in the woods, but it was a chance she would rather take. The clearing in front of the house was likely kept under surveillance. In that case, it would be better to go in the dark when a camera would be hampered by the limited range of the night vision spectrum. By the time she figured out if there was an infrared camera it would be too late. Her heat silhouette would definitely not look like a deer or coyote. This was another chance she would have to take if she wanted to find a position where she could talk to Jirafa alone.

Looking again at the satellite map of the property she believed to be Jamie Jordan's house, there was no visible fenceline in the woods, but there appeared to be a trail from the lake to the crossover at the highway she spotted during her drive-by. Hopefully the trail continued on to the house.

María slept for a couple of hours, waking long before dawn to eat the remainder of the snacks Isabella packed for the trip. The drive to the lake was peaceful in the pre-dawn hour. Finding the trail on the side of the parking lot, she entered the woods. With only the light of a quarter moon and one small flashlight, this would be a tricky navigation, but María's experience and instincts kicked in.

Crossing the highway, María found the trail again on the other side. There were several pairs of snake eyes and animals making rustling noises in the woods, none of which fazed her. The trail stopped at a gravel lane, presumably the one between the houses. Because of the tree canopy overhead and narrow sides, the lane was likely unmonitored.

Gravel crunched under María's feet as she proceeded left toward the house with the pool. Switching off the flashlight, the eerie glow of the whitish gray stones under the dim moon filtering through the trees was the only light to navigate by.

As María reached the edge of the clearing for the house, she heard a sound in front of her. An outdoor light came on and the flash of a deer's white tail disappeared into the woods.

"Mmm, a motion sensor," María mouthed quietly to herself.

After one minute, the light turned off. María doubted whoever lived in the house wanted a floodlight to come on every time a skunk crossed the road or a deer grazed through the yard. The light would be flashing on and off all night in a place like this. She picked up a large stick and threw it into the clearing, low across the road. A dull *thump* but no light. She picked up another stick and threw it about five feet off the ground in the same path. The light came on.

"Okay, no sudden movement and stay low." María crouched, proceeding slowly along the side of the lane until she was within what she calculated to be surveillance camera range. At this point she veered to the right, making her way toward the back of the house. She wanted a view of the layout of the house, looking for a place Jirafa was most likely to appear at daylight. María hoped to catch Jirafa's attention and steal a few minutes alone with her to talk. Hopefully Jirafa could protect her from whatever security subsequently descended on her unexpected arrival, or she could disappear back into the woods.

In the moonlight María saw the shimmer of the pool and a person lying on a lounge chair on the patio. She crept slowly and cautiously toward the figure. This could be a security guard, asleep on the job.

Fortunately, no security light illuminated as María stepped onto the patio. The person on the chair seemed to be asleep, curled slightly to one side with arms behind the head. This was exactly how Jirafa slept.

With the first light of day barely making an appearance over the house, María began to make out the face of the person a few feet from her. It was definitely Jirafa, characteristically sleeping outside. María silently crouched on one knee next to the chair.

A deep bark came from the other side of the chair. Boo barely opened her eyes. "Fred, shhhh."

Sensing someone next to her, Boo startled awake as the dark figure put a hand over her mouth and a strong hand clasped her arm.

"Jirafa, it's me."

María's voice was enough. Boo reached up to take the hand from her mouth.

"María—what? How? Where?" Boo could only manage one word questions as she rolled over and grabbed María into a tight clinch that looked more like a tackle causing Fred to bark again.

"Fred, shhhh." Boo looked at María, attempting to focus on her face. "Why are sneaking around in the dark? Let's go inside where I can see you." She started to stand but María held her down.

"No, we need to talk. The police are looking for us, for you."

"Yes, I can explain." Boo shook her head to gather her thoughts, but having awoken from a deep sleep, she was not quick enough.

The unmistakable sound of a gun cocking behind María's head pierced the still morning air.

"Don't move or I will kill you," Jamie emphasized the word *will*. "Now, take your hands off Boo, get on your stomach, arms out to the side." Jamie had learned the command from a movie script and it seemed apropos for the situation.

This was perhaps Jamie's best acting ever. The gun in her hand was a prop from a movie, brought home as a souvenir. She kept it secretly locked away, hidden from Max because she did not want him to think a gun was a toy.

"María, don't hurt her," Boo spoke calmly, fearing the worst. "Jamie, please, don't shoot. It's María."

"María?" Jamie lowered the gun.

"Boo? Jirafa, who's Boo?" María was more interested in the name than the gun. She jumped to her feet.

"Jirafa? Who's Jirafa?" Jamie was as perplexed as María at this point.

"I'm Boo, and I'm Jirafa." Boo had recognized her nickname the second María spoke it. "María, what's my real name?"

Confusion overtook María's face. "What do mean, what's your real name? It's—"

A figure flew out of the dark, tackling María and propelling both of them into the pool. Surfacing several feet apart, Fred jumped into the water between them, breaking their focus on each other. Startled, Jamie dropped the gun, causing a blank shot to fire. Everyone stopped.

"Sarah, it's María. It's okay." Jamie beckoned her sister to the near side of the pool.

María took a few short backstrokes to the opposite side of the pool, distancing herself from Sarah and Jamie but never taking her eyes off of them. Boo joined her.

"It's a blank, it's not a real gun. I'm not going to shoot you," Jamie yelled across the pool to reassure María and Boo.

María took the statement as a cue to pull herself out of the pool and stand next to Boo. The two pairs stood on opposite sides of the pool looking wearily at each other. Fred walked up the steps at the end of the pool and shook vigorously, spraying water everywhere, momentarily distracting everyone from their stand-off.

"What is going on here?" Sarah demanded.

"Me caen bien." María's eyes twinkled as she flashed a wide grin at Boo. "I'm starting to really like these two."

Chapter Twenty-three

DUCKING INSIDE THE back door to the house, Jamie grabbed a couple of pool towels. She handed one to Sarah, then walked around the pool to where Boo and María stood. Jamie offered María a towel.

"Hi, I'm Jamie. I don't believe we've been formally introduced."

"I'm María. Sorry, I didn't mean to scare you. I just need to talk to Jirafa...I mean Boo."

"That's Sarah, my sister. She doesn't usually greet people like..." Jamie let the thought hang, certain Sarah would do it again if she thought anyone in the family was in danger.

"Hi," Sarah offered, "I was out for a morning run and heard a voice I didn't recognize. I thought someone..." The rest of the thought seemed self-explanatory given her actions.

"Okay," María turned to Boo, "I need for you to explain this all to me, but first, we need to talk. Alone. Please?"

"Just for the record, are we married?" Boo's face was pained and confused.

"What? Yes, we are. Hopefully not much longer." Realizing her words sounded unkind, María quickly added, "I don't mean it that way—just a couple of minutes, then you can go back to whatever is going on here." María's patience was giving way to annoyance.

They all turned their heads as a car slid to a halt at the side of the house. Bryan ran onto the patio to Sarah's side. "What's going on? I thought I heard a gunshot. You didn't answer your phone. Is everyone okay? Why are you wet?" Then, realizing there was a stranger on the patio, he demanded, "Who's that?"

"Is this the whole family, or are there more surprises coming at me?" María asked Boo.

"Not quite everyone, and hopefully not," Boo replied with a shrug.

"Who are you? Is everyone okay?" Bryan's body shook from the adrenaline rush.

"We're all fine. This is the María we've been looking for. Boo's spouse," Jamie spoke slowly, still not sure of the whole story. "There seems to have been a misunderstanding. We're trying to sort it all out."

"Would you all excuse us, please?" Boo asked across the pool before looking at María and nodding her head toward the doors to her bedroom in the house.

"Ah, I better not. I'm still dripping. How about we head over there?" María walked toward the far side of the patio, placing as much distance as possible between herself and the unpredictable, jumpy family standing next to the house.

"How did you find me?" Boo asked.

"A federal agent came looking for me to find you. I didn't want to talk to her until I found out what is going on. I saw your picture online, but you didn't answer your phone or text or email. Qué, Jirafa?"

"It's a long story—"

"Okay, we don't really have time for that right now. Any idea why the feds are looking for you?"

"That's what I'm trying to tell you. The short version is—I hit my head, I lost my memory, someone stole my backpack with everything in it, I don't remember my own name. The police are trying to help me figure it out. I did remember you, so we were trying to find you."

María blinked several times while she realized the full implications of Boo's story.

"You remembered me but you don't remember your own name?"

"Exactly—"

Boo was interrupted by Chief walking briskly around the side of the house. Her right hand rested on her holstered gun as she assessed the scene. Jamie, Sarah, and Bryan were huddled by the door to the house. There was a stranger with Boo. Two people were dripping wet and wrapped in towels. Fred, also wet, lay between the groups as if to keep them separated.

"Would someone like to explain what's going on here?" Chief ordered more than inquired.

"It's okay. This is María. We're just talking," Boo offered.

"We received a 911 call but no one was on the line. Then dispatch thought they heard a gunshot." Chief spotted the gun on the patio. "Jamie, what happened here?"

"It's not a real gun, it's a prop. I dropped it and a blank fired. I'm sorry." Jamie flushed with embarrassment. "Everything is okay. We're glad María is here." Jamie was diplomatic despite the remaining confusion surrounding the early morning stealth visit by Boo's spouse.

Chief walked to where Boo and María stood, extending a hand to María as a gesture of goodwill. "Hi, I'm the Sheriff. Would one of you want to explain...any of this?"

"Ah, the Sheriff. I've heard about you," María observed.

Boo addressed the question, "If you would please give us a couple of minutes, we will clear this up. I promise. María came a long way to find me."

Chief called an all clear to dispatch and walked toward the house, handing Sarah her cell phone from the driveway and ushering Jamie and Sarah inside. Bryan left for home, leaving Boo and María alone on the patio.

"Your name is Kele—Kele Severin Garcia. You took my last name when we married."

"I remember now. My grandmother named me Kele. You called me Jirafa, because I'm taller than you, a girafe. I remember." Boo eyes filled with tears of relief.

"Jirafa," María used the nickname with affection, "why are they calling you Boo?"

"It's a nickname Max gave me after I saved him. It seemed like as good a name as any," Boo raised her eyebrows and shrugged.

"Okay, Boo," María used the new nickname with slight exaggeration, "back to the beginning. Who's Max? How did you hit your head? Feel free to start anywhere." There were a lot of holes in the story needing to be filled in.

Boo summarized the tale of the past three weeks of her life, leaving out the part about falling in love with Jamie. She concluded with what they believed to be the failed search for María.

"Wow, obviously we had no idea. We thought you were off the grid working. We worried when the fed showed up. I was afraid we were in trouble," María responded.

"Why would we be in trouble with the police?" Boo asked. "Chief searched my fingerprints and said I didn't have an arrest record or anything."

"You haven't done anything wrong. Neither of us has. It has to do with immigration."

"Your family, tu mamá y tu papá—are they okay?" Boo remembered helping María's parents move from Mexico to settle into their new home with Miguel. "Miguel and his family—I remembered them. Is everyone okay?"

"Yes, everyone is fine. You're the only one we're worried about. We thought our divorce might set off questions about whether our marriage was real. I thought the feds were looking for you to ask questions, trying to make it look like we committed fraud. I didn't want them to accuse you of anything. It seems like they are actively trying to hurt people now."

"So, Chief's friend did find you? But she said you were married to someone else." Boo searched her memory. "You're married to Isabella? But we're still—"

"No, I'm not married to Isabella, yet. You and I are still married and we're supposed to finalize our divorce next week, so Isabella and I can get married. I just let the neighbor woman the fed talked to think Isabella and I are married. Miss Miriam is all up in everyone's business. If she thought Isabella and I were not married, she would be all over me about living in sin and making Isabella an honest woman. Honestly, I didn't know people even still talked like that until I met Miss Miriam."

Boo laughed at her fearless spouse, frightened by a busybody neighbor.

"So, we are getting divorced? Next week? How long have we been split up?"

"For years, sort of. We drifted apart, we broke up, we stayed living together...I guess we're really good lesbians. We had a house. Plus, you promised when we first got together to help me bring my family to the States, and you never break a promise. You have been very good to them." Now María's eyes teared thinking of the sacrifices Boo made for her family.

"What about my family? Do I have a family? I thought I remembered a brother and a nephew."

"Yes, your brother Tomas, his wife Yura, and your nephew, Michael, live in Alaska. You don't see them very often. Your mother and father both passed away a couple of years ago." María put hand on Boo's arm. "I'm sorry. You were estranged from them for a long time."

It was Boo's turn to have tears in her eyes. She remembered the separation from her parents, but not the reasons why.

"I remembered your name and I remembered I fucked up our relationship. I remember putting work ahead of you. I'm sorry." Boo saw this as her chance to atone for past behavior.

"It's all water way under the bridge. We worked through all that and we're friends—you're the most loyal person I have ever met. You could have moved on with your life, but you stuck it out to make sure my family was taken care of.

I don't begrudge you working hard when half the time you were supporting me so I could finish my degree, and you helped support my family."

"I think we need to explain." Boo looked toward the house, seeing Jamie and Chief standing inside by the kitchen window. "Ready?"

"Yes. Is it safe to talk in front of the Sheriff?" María asked, weary of police.

"Chief? Yes, she's a friend. She really is."

"Do you want to ask anything else before we go in?"

Boo looked back at the window framing a worried looking Jamie. "If I wanted to ask someone, like, on a date, when will I be available, as in not married?"

"You should ask her now," María followed Boo's eyes to the window. "You are available. You have been for a long time. We'll just make it official next week."

Boo and María entered the house through the doors to Boo's room first for María to dry off and change into the clothes Boo offered. Unfortunately, María's phone had been ruined by the dunk in the pool. She borrowed Boo's phone to call Isabella and assure her everything has gone as planned, more or less, and promising to explain everything soon.

Boo and María walked into the kitchen to the expectant looks of Jamie and Chief. Sarah joined them, dressed in dry clothes borrowed from Jamie's closet. They all took seats around the kitchen table.

"Who wants to go first?" Chief asked the assembled group.

"I will. I'm sorry I scared you all by sneaking in. I thought I needed to protect...Boo," María was still adjusting to the new nickname. "I wanted to talk to her privately and she wasn't answering her phone or text. We were very worried about her."

"I'm sorry, too." Sarah pursed her lips in thought. "Well, not really. I thought someone was trying to hurt Jamie and Boo." Sarah was not the least bit contrite, but managed to add with sincerity, "I hope I didn't hurt you."

"I guess we were both trying to protect people we care about. No harm done. Well, except my phone." María admired the fiercely protective, unapologetic woman across the table from her.

"Okay, Boo, it's your turn." Jamie's face mixed concern with curiosity.

"My name is Kele Severin Garcia. I was born in Colorado. I have a brother, sister-in-law and nephew in Alaska. Both of my parents are deceased. I am married to María, but we are finalizing our divorce next week, so María can marry the lovely Isabella." A feeling of satisfaction settled over Boo, who was relieved to finally have a name. She turned to María. "Where do I live?"

"You moved to upstate New York a couple of months ago. We sold the house we owned together. Isabella and I bought a place and you moved in across town from us. You wanted to be close to the kids—"

"Kids?" Everyone in the room raised their eyebrows in shock.

"Zoe and Roxie? The kids?" Seeing the misunderstanding, María added, "They're cats. Two big fluffy, old, sweet cats. We share custody. Okay, we are total lesbians."

Everyone at the table laughed and sighed with relief.

"Whew, I remember. I dreamed I was looking for them. It was one of the first dreams I had."

The group heard a vehicle pull up to the front of the house and three car doors close. Within seconds, Max burst through the front door.

"Mom! Boo!" Max bounded toward them, throwing himself into Boo's arms. Lessa and Philip followed close behind.

Boo looked over the top of Max's head at María.

"Almost the whole family now."

Chapter Twenty-four

"BRYAN TEXTED US ABOUT María. I hope you don't mind if we join you. We don't want to miss this." Lessa approached María with an outstretched hand. "Hi, I'm Lessa, Jamie and Sarah's mother, and Max's grandmother."

Philip offered his hand and introduction next.

"And this is Max," Boo said, tousling the boy's sleepy brown hair. "Max, this is my very, very good friend, María."

"Hi, Max. I've heard about you. Es un placer conocerte." María winked at Max.

"Hi." Max, holding onto Boo, gave María a shy look through his long eyelashes.

"Don't let us interrupt the conversation." Lessa raised her eyebrows to indicate her acute interest.

"How about breakfast and tea while we continue?" Jamie offered. She and Boo rose from their chairs at the same time to belatedly begin the morning routine.

"Chief, will you join us?" Boo asked.

"I should head back to the office." Chief sensed María's distrust of law enforcement officers. "I assume you will fill me in later. Unless I'm missing something, this case seems to be wrapping up." Chief stood to leave, adding, "It is a pleasure to meet you, María. I'm very glad we found you. If you don't mind, I will let my friend know she did find the right person after all."

"That would be fine, Chief. I'm pleased to meet you, too."

"Do I have a job? Why am I in Crestwood?" Boo began her inquisition of María.

"You are an ecosystem ecologist," María explained, "you have a PhD and own your own consulting business, protecting and restoring native areas. I'll show you your website later. You were on your way to conduct a couple of field studies. When you'll be in the field for a long time, you catch a ride so you won't have to find a place to leave your truck. You were dropped off at the diner on the north side of Crestwood, but we never found the person who was supposed to pick you up. The people at the field site thought your schedule changed and you would show up later. We all expected you to be out of touch and no one realized you were missing. We would have figured it out next week when you were scheduled to return."

The fruit, eggs, and bagels on the table were absent mindedly consumed as everyone listened intently to Boo and María.

"Why would you think the feds would care about our divorce?" Boo asked the question innocently, causing María to shift uncomfortably in the chair.

"I became US citizen last year." María weighed how to answer in front of everyone. She decided on a short summary, hoping it would be enough to jog Boo's memory. "The government finally recognized our marriage. We thought they might be looking into our divorce, as though the marriage was not real."

"They can't take away your citizenship, can they?" Boo asked. "Just because we're divorcing?"

"No, they can't take it back," Lessa offered. "You two are legally married and obviously it is what they call, in quotes, a real marriage. You are allowed to divorce." Lessa addressed María directly, "I'm an attorney. I provide services for the women at the emergency and residential shelters. One of the issues we deal with is immigration status. A lot of women don't want to report abuse because they are afraid of being deported. I won't deny it happens, unfortunately, but I have worked with attorneys here and in Fairfield to learn as much as possible about the law. We try to help these women leave abusive partners, and stay and work in the US. Most of the women have children they are trying to support. I'm sorry you have to worry about your status."

María relaxed, feeling more at ease discussing her situation.

"I'm nervous because we hear the horror stories about families being torn apart. Some people are sent to places where they haven't lived in decades, if ever. And my family—we brought them to the US from northwest México where there has been a lot of gang violence. We were afraid for their safety. Boo helped my brother through college in the US—she paid for it. Then she helped him find a job so he could stay. After my abuelos all passed, we brought my parents too. I do not want any of this to affect them."

"If I can help, please do let me know." Lessa reached across the table to squeeze María's hand.

Not counting the initial reception by Sarah, María was touched by the kindness of the family. Although, even Sarah's reception was touching too, in dangerous sort of way.

Jamie had texted Shon earlier and invited them to join the group. Shon arrived at the house, coming in the front door and following the noise to the kitchen.

"I knew I found the right María Garcia." Shon wrapped María in a welcoming hug. "Back to the beginning. Boo, who are you and why were we separated at birth?"

María was quickly acclimating to the family dynamics and interplay. Everyone chimed in, with dozens of questions flowing over an extended breakfast. The numerous stories of Boo's exploits, both before and after her arrival in Crestwood, embarrassed her. Bryan eventually rejoined the family with Marco and Gee in tow. What had started as a tense morning standoff around the pool became more like a family reunion.

With María's prompting, Boo remembered more missing pieces of her life. The sudden flood of memories of places, people, and events overwhelmed her. Jamie saw the glazed look creeping across Boo's face.

"Hey, why don't we take a break," Jamie interjected. "I think we should give Boo a little time to digest all of this. Would someone take María to retrieve her car, please? María, you may use the front gate this time. I would like for you to stay here with us." Jamie smiled invitingly at Boo's soon to be ex-spouse. She wanted María to feel welcome, and for Boo to not feel as though she had to choose whether to stay with Jamie or go with María. At least not yet.

Sarah and Bryan took the kids home while Lessa and Philip headed back to town, dropping María at her car along the way. Max retreated to his room to find special paper for a drawing for María. Boo and Jamie were left standing in the kitchen.

"I'm happy for you, Boo. Just let me know how I can support you." Jamie put on a brave face.

"Thank you. I guess I need to go back to my home and find out what I remember. To be honest, I feel overwhelmed. It's only been three weeks but it feels like my life has been totally upended all of a sudden." Boo looked at Jamie as if asking an unvoiced question.

"Do what you need to do," Jamie closed the distance between them, embracing Boo and whispering, "nothing has changed for me. I want you in my life and in Max's life. I want you to be part of my family. I don't want to be selfish, but I do want you to understand how much you mean to me."

"I want all of that, too." Boo inhaled the scent of Jamie's warm body. "Is it okay if it takes a little while to figure out?"

"Yes."

Boo and Jamie held each other, neither daring to let their hands, or lips, roam free. Not yet at least.

"May I help you clean up this impromptu mess?" Boo asked, stepping back from their embrace.

"Take a walk. I'll take care of this."

Boo collected Max and Fred for their daily hike through the woods. Max happily skipped along, talking about the museum and asking how soon they could make a return visit. Boo, not wanting to make a promise she could not keep, did not answer.

María reappeared in the kitchen a short time later, as Jamie finished cleaning the counters and loading the dishwasher.

"May I help with something?" María offered.

"Thanks, I'm almost done. Please, have a seat." Jamie motioned toward the table. "Would you like something to eat or drink?"

"No, thank you, I'm fine. I really appreciate you inviting me to stay here, given the whole stealth thing this morning." María settled into a chair. "Boo...is it okay if I call her Boo? Should I call her Jirafa? I don't want to disrespect your relationship with her."

"Boo is fine. I rather like it. I think maybe she has grown out of Jirafa, in a manner of speaking."

"Boo is out for a walk with Max and Fred. I think she needed a little fresh air and some semblance of normality—at least as she has come to know it here."

"Boo is surprisingly habitual for someone who goes off the grid for weeks at a time. She's also surprisingly habit-forming," María offered her first attempt at signaling that she could see the relationship forming between Boo and Jamie.

"Is it too personal for me to ask if Boo seems the same to you? We had no way to assess whether she changed in any way after she hit her head."

"She seems the same. She is unassuming, very compassionate, but can be reserved. All of that seems the same. The one difference is I have never seen her this...content. She focuses a lot of her energy and tends to bury herself in work. But she seems relaxed here. Happy. It's good to see her this way."

"Admittedly, the situation here has been...I don't know what to call it, it's not artificial...not contrived...maybe, protected. I was trying to give her a space to feel connected and grounded while she recovered."

"You have succeeded. She's obviously very attached to you and your family. It reminds me of her attachment to my family. She has always done her best to be there for them."

"I'm sorry if I'm asking private questions. Just tell me if you don't want to answer. I am curious though, because Boo seemed to have no idea who I am. I don't want to sound conceited, but most people do recognize me." Jamie did not doubt Boo's word, but she still wondered if the lack of recognition was a result of the amnesia.

"Boo rarely sits still. She doesn't watch much TV at all. She doesn't even own one. She's not on the computer except to work. The only movies I remember her seeing were when she took our nephew to kid's movies. It's not likely she recognized you."

"She remembered a couple of animated movies I voiced for."

"Movies may seem a bit frivolous to her." María instantly regretted her choice of words, "I mean...I'm sorry. I'm not criticizing your work. She definitely appreciates the arts and creativity."

"It's okay," Jamie let María off the hook, "a lot of people think movies are frivolous or escapism at best. I feel the same way about most of them, even some of the films I've been in."

"In case you haven't noticed, I'm pretty straight-forward. I can see Boo is very fond of you. She looks at you in a way...well, I've never seen her look at anyone that way. I don't want to see her get hurt."

"I don't know if there is anything I can say to make you trust I don't want to hurt her. I want quite the opposite." Jamie resisted telling María she was in love with Boo before she broke the news to Boo herself.

"I'm sure you have...well, let's just say, a lot of women who would like to hook up with you." María's face was as serious as her tone, "If Boo is just one of a string of women—"

Jamie cut her off, "After this morning, I'm pretty sure I don't want to find out the consequences."

Jamie and María nodded their mutual appreciation and understanding.

"Jamie, if you are serious about Boo, you need to tell her. She has not pursued possible relationships in the past because she wouldn't divorce me. Fortunately for me, Isabella is totally wonderful and understanding. She gets it. But it's time for Boo to move on. We will be divorced by the end of next week. I think you're the one who could be the reason for her to move forward with her life."

Jamie looked down at the table to avoid María's eyes for a moment while she composed her thoughts. Boo and Max saved her from replying as they bounded in the door.

Max took a seat by María, regaling her with stories from the morning walk.

"Did I miss anything?" a refreshed Boo inquired.

Chapter Twenty-five

BOO AND MARÍA SAT ON the patio reminiscing while Jamie and Max made a trip to town for groceries.

"I need to drive back home tomorrow. I also need for you to be back next week sometime to finalize the divorce." For the first time in a long while, María could not read the emotions of her dear friend.

"I'll come with you. I need to come back to my home and figure out where to pick up with my life," Boo responded with a mixture of resignation and determination.

"Jirafa, I'm going to stop you right there," María reverted to Boo's old nickname out of habit. "It's not really your home. You only moved because it's where Isabella and I want to be. You can do your job from anywhere. Your other friends and family are scattered everywhere. There's no reason you have to be there. Maybe you needed something big like this to happen to shake you up and move you forward. This seems more like your home now."

"But I really need to see what I can remember about my life. The doctor said I have to remember as much as I can as quickly as possible, otherwise the memories might be lost forever."

"Okay, you'll come with me tomorrow, but then you are coming back here to Jamie, and Max, and everyone else, if I have to tie you up and bring you myself."

Boo laughed as she did not doubt for an instant María would make good on her threat.

• • • •

JAMIE AND MAX FINISHED their shopping and dropped by Lessa and Philip's house to retrieve Max's bag, which had been forgotten in the morning's excitement.

"How are you, honey?" Lessa read the mixed feelings on Jamie's face.

"I'm fine. I..." Jamie could not think how to finish the sentence.

"This does not mean you are losing Boo. We have to support her through this. She needs to find her identity to move on in her life. I know that doesn't feel comforting right now, but it will all work out."

"What if she goes back and realizes she doesn't want to be in our lives? Maybe she will be happy to settle back into the way things were for her."

"Honey, this is really hard. She has needed you. Now you two need to transition to wanting to be together. I know you love her and it's scary," Lessa would declare Jamie's love for Boo even if Jamie did not have the courage to, yet. "This has to happen for you both to move forward. You couldn't do that until now."

"You're right. I need to be brave. I need to let her go. More than that, I need to support her going." The thought of Boo leaving brought the sting of tears to Jamie's eyes. She wanted to have as much faith in love as her mother did.

When Jamie and Max arrived home, Boo and María had lunch waiting for them. Jamie felt a twinge of jealousy watching how Boo and María interacted with each other. It was a familiarity she hoped she would one day enjoy with Boo.

In the afternoon, Boo and Max took María for a walk in the woods. Boo identified several rare plants, while María showed Max different animal tracks, caught two species of frogs, and spotted a couple of skink lizards scurrying around on a downed tree log. Max was quite enamoured with his newest friend.

As María and Max cleaned up from their adventure, Boo found Jamie sitting on the patio.

"Mind if I join you? I feel like I haven't seen much of you today." Boo sat on the chair next to Jamie.

"It has been a whirlwind. How are you feeling?"

"More and more memories are coming back to me. María says things and suddenly I remember. It's exciting and exhausting. I finally feel like I'm getting my life back."

"Have you given any thought to what comes next?" Jamie was doing her best to sound supportive despite her fears.

"I will drive back with María tomorrow. Apparently I have two jobs I was supposed to be finishing these past three weeks. I need to figure out what's going on and if there is some way I can still do the work." Seeing through Jamie's attempt at a brave face, Boo added, "I will be back. Soon. I promise."

María's words about Boo always keeping her promises reverberated through Jamie's mind. Jamie needed to believe those words right now.

"How can I help? What do you need?" Jamie wanted to offer money, a private jet, or to go with her, but she knew Boo was too independent to accept any of those.

"I can't think of anything. I'll need a new driver's license and credit cards, that kind of stuff. Then I'll figure out how to pay you back for everything—all the money you've spent on clothes and taking care of me. Good news is María says I'm still on her health insurance until we file the final divorce papers. And I've signed up for a new plan. I just have to find the information for the hospital." A multitude of details whirled through Boo's mind.

A lot was left unspoken between Boo and Jamie as they silently contemplated the coming days, but now did not seem to be the time to start a new conversation.

Max broke the silence by running through the doorway and jumping on his mother.

"I'm hungry."

"Again? I guess we better find some supper." Jamie snuggled Max for a moment. She looked over the top of Max's head at Boo, who was watching them intently. Jamie hoped this was enough to bring Boo back.

Supper was a subdued meal. Most of the obvious questions had been asked and many of the obvious stories had been told. Their separation weighed heavily on both Jamie and Boo as Max entertained María with stories about the children's museum. Toward the end of the meal, Boo explained to Max why she was leaving and promised to return soon.

"No. I want to come with you," Max whined.

Boo lifted Max out of his chair, taking him outside for a private talk.

"See the sun over there? Whenever the sun is up, I want you to think, Boo sees the same sun too. And when you see the moon come up, I want you to think, Boo sees the same moon too. I have to go and I will miss you. And because I will miss you so much, I will have to come back very soon."

"I'll miss you. When will you be back?" Max put his arms around Boo's neck and rested his head against hers.

"We will talk once a day, for fifteen minutes, and soon I'll be here again. While I'm gone, I need for you to spend time with your mom and Fred and your grandparents, and everyone you love. That will make the time go by quicker. Okay?"

"Okay. Can we have ice cream now?" Max's mood brightened.

Boo took Max back in the house, heading directly to the freezer. She looked across the room at Jamie, who had tears in her eyes, and decided she would need to have a similar talk with Jamie later.

The evening included phone calls to update Isabella, Gabriela, and Chief. At Max's bedtime, Jamie read him the first story, Boo another, and then he requested a story from María.

"I need the practice for when Isabella and I have kids," María smiled at the thought.

After storytime, María excused herself to Boo's bedroom to retire for the night. Boo followed her. Out of Jamie's hearing, María eyed Boo intensely.

"If you crawl in bed with me tonight or sleep on that patio, you better have a damn good excuse about why you are not in bed with the woman you love and who loves you back."

"How can I do that then leave in the morning? I don't want to hurt Jamie."

"You'll figure it out. Now get out of here. I want to sleep," María playfully pushed Boo out of the room and shut the door.

Boo walked through the kitchen to the patio. The sun had set on a peaceful June evening. Jamie soon wandered outside to sit beside her.

"Do I need to give you the same talk I gave Max?" Boo smiled gently at Jamie.

"Maybe. I'll miss you terribly."

"I'll miss you, too. But we will talk, at least once, probably a lot more, every day. And I know you have work to do and lots of family time."

"You really don't need to give me a pep talk, but I appreciate it." Jamie studied Boo's face in the glow of the kitchen light. "Your wife seems to think you should be cheating on her while you still have the chance."

"She actually shoved me out of the bedroom." Boo paused. "Jamie, I don't want to start something and then leave in the morning. I want to start something when...when I can be here, after I have found all of me. I want to share all that with you."

"In a way, isn't that what we have been doing? We both just forgot everything else for a while and were our real selves with each other?"

"And now we need to bring all the other stuff back in. We are whole people. Some of it is messy, and some is busy and chaotic, and that's what will make the choice to be together feel right. Not like we are forgetting everything else, but we see it all and choose each other."

A sprinkle of rain fell on the two women as lightening lit the sky above the clouds in the distance.

"Come on, you can't sleep outside tonight unless you want me to throw a tarp over you." Jamie was only half teasing. Knowing Boo, there was a good chance she would stay outside in the rain to avoid temptation. But temptation was exactly what Jamie had in mind.

Taking Boo's hand, Jamie pulled her off the chair and led her into the house. Jamie locked the door behind them. Keeping a hold on Boo's hand, Jamie walked them into her bedroom. She locked that door, too, in case Max woke up during the night and decided to pay a visit to his mother's room.

The only light illuminating the room came from a nightlight in the adjoining bathroom. It barely broke the darkness. Jamie moved to face Boo, hands intertwined, their bodies a mere inch apart.

"Your wife told me I should seduce you. Well, not in so many words..." Jamie felt the increasing warmth of Boo's body seep into her skin.

"Usually that would be a real mood killer, but in this case..." Boo replied, smiling at María's meddling.

"I want to kiss you now, Boo Charming." Jamie shifted slightly to close the gap between them, pressing her body against the full length of Boo's, her lips a breath from Boo's. "Is that okay?"

"Yes." Boo's resolve was totally vanquished by the radiant heat of Jamie's body.

Jamie pulled Boo's head down slightly until their lips met. The sensation was softer than any she had imagined or dreamed. As their lips parted slightly, the space became a vacuum, sucking them back into each other. Tongues met in an unforgettable taste of the sweetness of aroused breath. Each inhaled the heated scent of the other.

"I'm taking off my shirt and then I want to take off your shirt. I want to feel your skin." Jamie pulled her head back slightly, "Is that okay?"

"Yes," seemed to be the only word in Boo's vocabulary.

Jamie slowly lifted her own shirt over her head and threw it to the side. As she lifted Boo's shirt, it caught on Boo's nose. Both grinned at the clumsiness of the first time.

Jamie pulled Boo back to her body, wrapping her arms around Boo's waist. Jamie could feel Boo's small breasts pressed to her chest just above her own nipples. She lightly rubbed her hands over Boo's side and back. Boo gently held the back of Jamie's head in one hand and shoulders with the other, pulling Jamie into a long kiss.

Rain falling on the roof sounded a steady drumbeat. Thunder rose from the distance as a flash of light illuminated the window.

"I'm taking off my shorts now. Then I want to remove yours. May I?" Jamie wanted to make sure this was what Boo wanted as much as she did.

"How about I remove my own shorts, and then yours? Is that okay?" Boo countered, not seeking control, but parity in the interaction.

"Mmmm, yes." It was Jamie's turn to consent.

Boo stepped back far enough to pull her shorts and boxers off, tossing them aside. She reached for Jamie's shorts. The sharp click that signaled the unsnapping of the top of Jamie's shorts was gratifying, but the zipper pull stuck halfway down. They both giggled.

"We make this look so easy in the movies." A stuck zipper could ruin an entire take when filming a love scene, however, this was one love scene Jamie would not mind doing over and over again, with or without a clothing malfunction.

Jamie jiggled the zipper loose, sliding it down. She allowed her shorts to fall around her ankles and kicked them off. Boo slid her hands over Jamie's underwear and then under the sides until she could work them down Jamie's legs. These were tossed aside also.

Now naked, their bodies met and lips came together again.

"What now?" Boo breathed into Jamie's ear as her body shivered in anticipation.

"I want to lay you down on the bed. Then I want to lay on top of you and kiss you, all over." Jamie moaned involuntarily as she played the scene in her mind. "Is that what you want too?"

Boo could barely mouth the word, *yes*, between her rapid breaths.

Keeping their bodies connected, Jamie moved Boo across the room until she could safely push her back onto the bed. Boo slid herself across the sheets until only her feet dangled off the edge. Jamie carefully climbed onto the bed and lowered herself on top of Boo's body. Placing one thigh between Boo's legs to spread them, Jamie dipped her head to start kissing at Boo's navel, working her way slowly up the center line of Boo's chest. When she reached Boo's neck, Jamie lifted her head to kiss Boo's lips as she rested the full weight of her body on Boo.

Boo wrapped her arms around Jamie, holding her tightly as their tongues did a hungry tango. Jamie's hands worked their way down Boo's sides as far as she could reach, then back up.

"I want to suck on your nipples. May I?" Jamie whispered against Boo's mouth.

"Yes." There was nothing Boo wanted more at this moment.

Jamie shifted her body to one side, allowing a hand to roam freely across Boo's stomach, feeling the smooth softness of skin over taught abs. Jamie kissed and sucked on one of Boo's hard nipples, tasting Boo's skin as she rolled the nipple between her tongue and teeth while her fingers applied a similar pressure to the other nipple. Then Jamie switched sides, wanting to bathe each nipple in her mouth.

Boo moaned with pleasure as her body trembled with expectation.

"I want to touch you, make love to you." Jamie's intention was clear, but she clarified anyway. "Now. Is that what you want?"

"Yes, please," Boo gladly begged for Jamie's touch.

Jamie moved her hand between Boo's legs. It took no time find the source of Boo's wetness.

"May I touch you here?" Jamie waited for Boo's reply.

"Yes." Boo's breathing was hard and fast.

Jamie was momentarily torn between taking her time and granting both of their desire as soon as possible. She intensified her stroking, guided by Boo's response.

Boo struggled to remember to be as quiet as possible as any sense of time and place left her. She felt Jamie's touch and allowed herself be carried along by the rhythm of Jamie's fingers. Boo's body pressed into Jamie's hand as she arched blissfully into the intense contractions of her orgasm.

Boo recovered quickly, using her strong body to gently rolling Jamie over onto her back. Boo's thighs slid between Jamie's and her muscled arms supported her as she hovered just above Jamie.

"Your turn," Boo hummed into Jamie's ear. She traced one of Jamie's nipples with her fingers. "I want to suck on your nipples. May I?"

"No."

Boo immediately withdrew her hand, but Jamie caught it, lowering Boo's hand between her open legs.

"I want you to touch me here. Now. Please?" Jamie's urgency needed no further explanation.

Making love was one skill Boo had definitely not forgotten.

Jamie pulled Boo's mouth over hers to muffle the moans as Boo's fingers slid inside her. Jamie felt every nerve ending tingle as Boo's thumb caressed her swollen clit, almost immediately taking her body into rolling waves of release.

As their breathing slowed, their lips remained together, tongues dancing. This was not a dream or fantasy. The feeling of coming together on what could be their last night, or their new beginning, was real.

Chapter Twenty-six

THE NEW DAWN FOUND Boo and Jamie still tangled in each other's arms, their legs entwined.

The light peeked in through the blinds as Boo stirred first. She lay quietly, luxuriating in the memory of each orgasm of the previous night. Reliving Jamie's sweet kisses was cut short as she remembered she needed to be up and ready to leave with María on their long drive.

Jamie's head rested on Boo's shoulder. Boo lightly caressed the side of Jamie's face, gently guiding it up toward hers. She kissed Jamie softly on the forehead, then her nose, and finally her lips.

Jamie moaned as her body twitched awake, caught between an erotic dream and immediate lustful urges. Her body buzzed with aroused nerves. Stretching to seek out the rest of Boo's body, Jamie breathed in the scent of sex still in the air from the previous night's activity.

"Mmmmm, I like waking up this way," Jamie pulled Boo closer.

"Mmmmm, me too. I'd like to...but we need to get out of bed, make some breakfast for Max and María." Boo sighed, kissing Jamie's delicious lips one final time.

Jamie and Boo reluctantly crawled from the bed, searching for clothes scattered about the room. Jamie washed her face and wanted to suggest a joint shower, but that would seriously delay their appearance in the kitchen. Max would be starved by the time they finished.

Boo and Jamie held hands as they walked into the kitchen. They were surprised to find Max and María there, quietly cooking breakfast. Neither Boo nor Jamie could contain a blush.

"Look what the cat dragged in," María gave the two a self-satisfied smile as she flipped an omelet in the pan.

"Look, Boo, María and I are making you and mom breakfast," Max stated with pride.

"Thank you, buddy. This looks great. I'm famished." Boo had worked up an appetite overnight.

"Thank you, mijo. This is very thoughtful. How long have you two been up?" Jamie was curious how María managed to keep Max quiet. Usually a mother's ears picked up on the sounds of a stirring child anywhere in the house.

"We wanted to surprise you!" Max was pleased the plan had worked.

"Did the thunder and lightning keep you two kids up late last night? You look a little sleep deprived." María was clearly enjoying teasing the new lovers.

"Nope, slept just great." Boo shook her head at María, not bothering to contain a guilty grin.

"I thought we would eat, then pack and head out. Jamie, I hope you don't mind if we leave early?" María, concerned about Jamie's feelings, wanted to include both Jamie and Max as part of the planned departure.

"Sooner you get on the road, the sooner you'll be back home with Isabella, and Roxie and Zoe." Jamie engaged her acting skills to cover her feelings of desperately wanting to hold onto Boo and not allow her to depart.

Breakfast included discussion of the planned trip as well as some of the upcoming events Jamie and her family had planned. Jamie made it clear that María and Isabella were welcome in her home at any time. "Without even a moment's notice," Jamie added with a wink.

After breakfast, María asked Max for help loading the bags and cooler in the car, giving Jamie and Boo a final moment alone together.

"I will be back." Boo tenderly pulled Jamie into an embrace, speaking directly into Jamie's ear, "I promise."

Jamie closed her eyes tight to prevent tears from spilling out. Releasing their hold on each other, they stoically walked outside. Boo hugged Max, leaving him with the same message of promised return.

As María drove along the driveway toward the highway, she glanced at Boo. Boo's eyes were not filled with tears as she expected. The golden brown eyes of her friend, and soon to be ex-spouse, were resolute, focused, and clear.

The drive to María and Isabella's house was long, giving Boo and María hours to talk. Boo asked questions and María told all of the stories she could remember about Boo's past. After their years together, María knew almost all there was to know about Boo's life. The stories helped to restore many memories as recognition led to recall, and recall led to connections to other memories.

"Did we ever want to have kids?" Boo wondered if her attachment to Max was a long time desire or something new.

"We talked about it. But with us both working and trying to bring my family here, it just never became a part of our plan."

"I can see having a family with Jamie. I hope I would be a good parent. I expect to be around for you and Isabella's kids."

"You'll be a great parent, and a great godmother," María assured Boo.

Boo drove for a couple of hours, giving María a break. Her driving skills were rusty, but quickly refreshed on the relatively quiet interstate. The duo passed the time by checking in with Isabella and Jamie, texting amusing pictures from the car.

"So, how was it last night?" María had waited as long as she could possibly stand before asking directly.

"It's a little weird telling my wife about sleeping with another woman." Boo ducked the question without expecting the dodge to work. After all, she now remembered that María had not been reticent about sharing details when she and Isabella started their relationship.

"Oh, get over yourself," María chided Boo.

"It was wonderful. Intense. Will it offend you if I say it was the best sex I've ever had? But it wasn't just sex, it was way more."

"I'll try to console myself by pretending you just don't remember the fabulous sex we had." María's exaggerated attempt to appear offended dissolved into a guffaw. "I'm happy for you. Really, truly happy. You deserve to find someone. I like Jamie, and Max, and the rest of the family. It's obvious how much they adore you. That makes me happy."

• • • •

PART OF JAMIE WANTED to do nothing except curl up on the bed and wallow in self-pity. Instead, she packed a lunch for herself and Max, and drove to town. She called her mother and father, asking if she and Max could join them for the day. She would work in the garden at the shelter house, fix bicycles, whatever they had planned. She needed the company of family, distraction, movement, activity—anything to keep her mind off Boo's leaving. She wanted someplace to hide from missing Boo and the fear she would never see Boo again.

Jamie found Philip at the shelter working in the garden with several of the women who were staying there. Max joined the other children at the small adjacent playground, while Jamie pulled weeds and staked tomato cages.

The women in the garden recognized Jamie. Their initial greeting was stand-offish, suspicious that her appearance among them was a publicity stunt. Their eyes roamed the surroundings searching for photographers or video cameras. When they realized this was not a photo op, and Jamie was just as sweaty and dirty as they were, they relaxed and included her in the conversation.

During lunch break, Jamie took a short walk, texting Boo, *Working in the garden with Dad and several wonderful women. Missing you a lot. Hope the trip is going well. Talk soon.* Hard physical work was good for ignoring the excitement in her body leftover from the previous night's activities, but she could not shake the wistful feelings Boo's absence created in her life.

After a long day laboring in the shelter garden, Jamie and Max joined her parents for dinner. She had little desire to go home to the empty guest room, the empty chair at the table, and the empty spot next to her in bed.

"Would you two like to stay here tonight? We can watch a movie? Eat ice cream?" Lessa's eyes made contact with her daughter's as if she could read her mind.

"That would be nice, Mom, but aren't you tired and busy?" Jamie was aware of her mother's real motivations.

"We're all tired, right Max?" Lessa pulled Max into the conversation, counting on her grandson to take her side.

Max looked at his mom with long lashes framing soft brown eyes.

"Okay, we'll stay." Jamie snuggled Max on one side of her on the couch as her mother sat close on the other side. "Thanks, Mom."

• • • •

AS THEY NEARED THEIR destination, Boo asked if she could spend the night with María and Isabella.

"I don't think I can face my place yet. Not alone." Boo was scared to enter her condo, not remembering anything about how it felt to be there. She was also afraid of falling back into old habits, forgetting Jamie and Max.

They parked and practically ran up the steps to the house. Isabella greeted Boo at the door as if she were a long lost puppy who journeyed thousands of miles to return home.

"Boo, I'm glad you're okay. You had us worried. Well, a lot of things had us worried, but mostly you." Isabella combed her fingers through Boo's short hair looking for the new scar.

"Thank you for supporting the rescue mission." Boo gave Isabella a wet kiss on the cheek to show her appreciation.

"From what I hear, you hardly needed rescue. More like...reminding. And you found someone special?" Isabella had heard all about Jamie and Boo's budding romance from María and could hear the excitement in Boo's voice on the phone when she talked about Jamie and Max.

"Yes, she is special," Boo cheeks burned red. "And Max, too." This was all Boo could say without prompting tearful eyes. She missed them already, causing renewed determination to put her life in order before returning to Crestwood.

"What can we do to help with your re-entry?"

"María has been telling me stories for the last couple of days. I may need you to provide a reality check. I suspect she may have exaggerated a little here and there for her own benefit." Boo winked at Isabella. "Seriously, would you two mind going with me to my place tomorrow? I can't do it alone right now."

Having never seen their friend feeling this vulnerable, María and Isabella nodded their agreement. Over dinner, plans for the next day were made.

Boo spent an hour after dinner on the couch scratching Roxie and Zoe's heads, listening to them purr. "I missed you two. I was searching for you in my dreams."

After Boo retired to the guest room, exhausted from the emotional stress of the journey, María and Isabella closed the door to their bedroom to process.

"She is obviously in love," Isabella observed. "The way she talked about Jamie during dinner...mmmm, mmm. How are we going to get those two together?"

"First, we will finalize the divorce. Then, we're packing up her condo, which should not be difficult because she has barely unpacked anything since she moved in. Then, we are driving her to Crestwood. She can sit in the front seat like a big girl, or we can box her up, too."

"Seems simple." Isabella smiled at how María's straightforward approach actually seemed to be the most sensible. "Any idea if she'll go along willingly?"

"That's not my problem." María laughed as she settled under the sheets, wrapping her soon-to-be wife in her arms.

· · · ·

JAMIE AWOKE EARLY FROM a restless sleep. She found her father sitting on the back porch, deep in his own thoughts.

"Morning, Dad. Thanks for letting me crash the garden party yesterday. Is there something I can help with today?"

"I was happy to have you. I think the women really enjoyed it too, once they started to trust you. It's hard for them to trust someone new." Philip worked hard to recognize his position around the women at the shelter and appreciate the difficult journey the women there were on.

Jamie often thought about how privileged her life was and what responsibilities came with that. The lessons she learned from her father and mother informed the way she raised Max. Those lessons were also influencing her plans for future work and family, which she hoped included Boo.

"Would you like to help with the Bikes-for-Kids rollout? We are planning a party to present the children with their new bikes weekend after next. We have a load of bikes to take to Fairfield to the shops and bring back the ones they have already repaired and reconditioned. Would you mind making the trip? Later, maybe you could help me with the party planning?" Philip proposed.

"Absolutely. Sounds like a plan. Time for breakfast and let's get this day started."

· · · ·

MARÍA AND ISABELLA slept in an hour later than usual. When they came down the stairs, Boo was in the kitchen cooking breakfast.

"Excuse me? What have you done with my Jirafa?...What?...You say she's been replaced by someone named Boo who can actually cook?" Isabella teased. "Well, I'll be...I like this new person."

"Seems I may have picked up a new skill or two," Boo blushed slightly, pleased with herself. The cats had been fed and Boo was enjoying being among friends who could help her remember her past, although cooking breakfast reminded her of mornings with Jamie and Max. Her heart ached as she thought about how much she missed them.

After breakfast, María and Isabella drove Boo to her condo. The short commute across town allowed Boo to recognize places along the way, although given the recent move, there was not much to remember.

Walking into the living room, as María predicted, was like walking into a storage unit. Boxes were stacked against the walls. The same was true of all the other rooms. The furniture, what little there was, sat where the movers had put it down. Clothes were still in bags and boxes, opened enough to find what Boo needed, but no more.

"Okay, this is rather depressing, but it will make it easier when we move you." María put her plan in motion.

"Move? Move where? I just got here," Boo protested.

"That's right. Don't get too comfortable. You are headed back to Crestwood as soon as we can hire a moving truck."

"What will I do there? I can't move in with Jamie. We don't even..." Boo realized she didn't know what was unknown.

"Blah, blah, blah. You own your own business, you can do your job from anywhere. Check. You have no ties here except me and Isabella and the cats. You'll visit us, we'll visit you. We'll send you pictures of the cats. La marca. You don't have to live with her. You have the money from selling the house. We'll find you a place. Check. You love this woman. You love her kid. You love her family. They love you. Check, check, la marca." María was on a roll. "Any questions?"

"Just one—how can you be certain she wants me to move there? It might be too soon." Boo wanted to take her relationship with Jamie seriously, making such a move seem presumptuous.

"Really? If it doesn't work out, what have you lost?" María pretended to wait for Boo to answer. "And if it does work out, then you'll thank us later, at the wedding. Your wedding."

"Whoa, that's way too fast," Boo resisted although she was surprised to realize she did not find the idea as scary as she might think she would. "You're right. I don't have anything to lose, and I have everything to gain. Would you two please help me figure this out?"

Isabella was impressed by how María brought Boo around in a matter of minutes. She enjoyed watching her soon-to-be wife use her powers for the forces of good. Now, if they could just keep Boo on track.

Chapter Twenty-seven

BOO SUBCONTRACTED ONE of her pending jobs and rescheduled the other for the following week. She needed to return to work to reestablish a sense of control over her life. She would have to take it slow for a while to avoid any reoccurring side effects of her concussion, but familiar activity would be comforting and restore a sense of normality.

Boo and María made the trip to the courthouse on Thursday morning to sign and file final paperwork for their divorce. To celebrate, Boo treated María and Isabella to dinner that evening.

"Now, you two crazy kids have to promise me you will not run off and get married without me. I have to give away at least one of the brides," Boo proclaimed.

"We promise, but you better have a plus one for the wedding. Kids allowed, so that's plus two," Isabella replied.

"We promise, no wedding without you. Have you talked to Shon about a finding a place in Crestwood?" María's task oriented nature surfaced.

"I can't think about it yet. It's just too soon in the relationship for such a big move. If there is a relationship," Boo talked herself into a spiral of doubt again.

"Nope, not going to happen. You will not let this one slip away." María had no intention of letting Boo undermine her master plan. "You love her, she loves you—"

"But she doesn't know the real me. What if she doesn't like this me? She's a big star. I'm sure there are lots of people she could have a relationship with. I'm just...me."

"Boo—and I will continue to call you Boo until you get the point—it doesn't matter what your name is or what you do for a living, it's you Jamie wants. This is you—kind, loyal, thoughtful, caring. Really, I just divorced you, are you going to make me go on and on about how wonderful you are?" María was prepared to do so, but hoped Boo would give in sooner rather than later.

"Boo, for once I agree with María's tactics." Isabella smiled at her soon-to-be wife's persistence. "You need to breathe and take a leap. From what I hear, you're willing to jump in front of a truck and off a cliff into a den of snakes. Moving to be with the woman you love has to be a lot less dangerous."

"You two make me sound wonderful, but I already screwed up my first marriage. That's what we're here celebrating, remember?" Despite being over the breakup and feeling great happiness for María and Isabella, Boo still felt that the end of the marriage was largely her fault.

"Boo, you are absolved. Don't make me talk about all of my faults in front of the woman who is about to take a leap of faith and marry me." María's patience was wearing thin. "No one is perfect. Except Isabella." María made adoring eyes at her flawless partner.

"Don't worry, sweetie, I am already well aware of your imperfections. It's part of what I love about you." Isabella took María's hand. "Boo, you've said before this is what you want—a family. I have never seen you to shy away from a challenge or run away from something because you're scared. Do you really want to start now?"

"You're both right." Boo, lost in thought, sat for a moment before continuing. "I need a plan. Otherwise I'll get comfortable here and tell myself my time with Jamie was a fairy tale that was too good to be true."

"Do you promise you'll talk to Shon? Better yet, text them right now. If you don't, I will," María's directive was more promise than idle threat, indicating her intention to closely monitor Boo's progress.

"Have you talked to Jamie? What does she say?" Isabella tried to moderate the conversation.

"I talk to her every day," Boo responded. "She wants a date when I'll be back, but she's obviously trying not to pressure me into anything."

"I'm driving. When do we pack and leave?" María wanted a timeline, too.

"Sweetie, chill a bit," Isabella reined in María's runaway train attitude. She reached across the table for Boo's hand. "When you met Jamie, you didn't know who she is or what her job is. You saw the person in front of you and you fell for her. She did the same thing. So, please, put your doubts aside. You are enough. She is enough. You have to give this love a chance."

"I appreciate your support. It means a lot to me." Boo pulled her shoulders back, sitting up tall. "I would like to be back in Crestwood within two weeks. First, I need to finish a job. I'll be gone for a couple of days."

"I'm putting a GPS tracker on you this time." María was taking no chances on losing Boo this time.

• • • •

JAMIE SCHEDULED A TRIP to New York City. Max would spend a couple of days with Sarah and Bryan and his cousins while she was away. Time in the city and work would take her mind off missing Boo. Jamie contemplated hiring a car and driving to Boo's home to surprise her, but resisted the urge. She wanted Boo to return of her own accord, without pressure. Jamie needed to be certain that returning to Crestwood was what Boo wanted. Besides, Boo had informed Jamie she would be out of touch for a couple of days while she finished a job in the field, leaving Jamie nervous and hoping this was not Boo's way of letting her down easy, breaking ties, and moving on.

When Jamie arrived at Gabriela's early in the week, they ordered delivery from their favorite pizza place and opened a bottle of wine.

"Remind me why we're sitting here instead of being on our way to find your one true love?" Gabriela was impatient with Jamie's equivocating.

"Because it needs to be Boo's choice."

"You think you have some magical power, if you just show up on her doorstep, she'll enter a trance and not be able to resist following you home? No free will at all? That sounds like a bad movie script to me. Hey, didn't you—" Gabriela began to tease Jamie about one of her less than stellar movie choices, but was cut off by Jamie's defense.

"Okay, no, I can't cast some magical spell over her. She obviously has her own mind. But what if she's decided it would be too much to live life under a microscope. Obviously it's not the life she's chosen."

"Everyone has stuff, baggage, whatever you want to call it. Yours just happens to be people who want to take pictures of you for some quick, dirty money. Once you two walk out in the sunshine, it will no longer be interesting. The paparazzi will find something more exciting to chase. You'll be a boring couple. Doesn't that sound wonderfully mundane?"

Jamie smiled at her friend's barely disguised disdain for the mundane parts of life that she herself cherished. She also appreciated what Gabriela was trying to tell her.

"Chief tells me the same thing. Have you two been talking?"

"Yes, that's how we spend our time after phone sex, talking about you and Boo." Gabriela winked at Jamie with a hint of delighted mischief in her eyes.

"Oh, I did not need to hear that," Jamie exaggerated her offense, shaking her head at Gabriela's antics, whether they were true or not. "Okay, I need to concentrate on work for the next couple of days. Then I'll have a heart-to-heart with Boo when she returns from her trip."

. . . .

JAMIE'S RENEWED ENERGY made the workdays in the city fly by. She felt good about what she accomplished before returning to Crestwood. Her future work plans were firming up and she looked forward to new challenges.

The rest of the week passed quickly. On Saturday morning, Jamie rose early to prepare for the Bikes-for-Kids event, driving to her parent's house to help with last minute details. Sarah and Bryan would bring Max and their kids later, in time for the main event. Chief had gathered free helmets and pads for each child receiving a bike. Shon helped with organization and set-up. Dani wrote a story about the program and today's roll-out. Gabriela designed T-shirts for the volunteers and a special T-shirt for the children. Everyone was pitching in to make this a memorable day for the children and their families.

In Jamie's mind, the only thing missing was Boo, who had been out of touch for five long days. The silence weighed on Jamie's mind.

The event began with a mid-morning brunch at the local park. The local bakery contributed a variety of muffins and juices, while vendors from the farmer's market donated fresh peaches and other in-season fruits. The diner on the north side of town brought fresh coffee and poured glasses of milk for the kids. It was a community event in every sense of the word.

Just before noon, Philip and Lessa made their way to a platform set up in front of the three large vans used to transport the bikes and equipment. Taking turns at the microphone, they thanked those responsible for making the event possible. Each registered child would receive a bike, safety equipment, and instruction. Rounds of applause showed the appreciation of the children, their families, and the community for the effort it took to create the program and make it a success.

Jamie's job for the event was to help Chief fit each child with a helmet and protective pads for their arms and knees. During the process, Jamie visited with the families and Max earnestly shook hands with each child.

After a child was fully outfitted in safety gear, the family walked across the platform to receive a bike. Volunteers rolled each bicycle from the back of one of the vans, staying with the child and their family for a short lesson in bicycle maintenance. Riding lessons followed for those who needed them.

After the last child was outfitted, Jamie and Chief began repacking the extra helmets and pads. Two volunteers rolled out the last bicycle onto the far side of the stage.

"Boo," Max yelled, bolting from Jamie's side to run across the platform and jump into Boo's outstretched arms.

Boo released the bike to the other volunteer just in time to catch Max.

"I've missed you," Boo told Max as she held him close, tousling his hair, and checking out his newly un-splinted hand.

Jamie looked up when Max yelled. It took her eyes a moment to adjust to the sight of the tall, dark haired woman holding her son and walking toward her. She glanced at Chief, who smiled in the way friends do when they just did something wonderful.

Jamie walked into Boo's outstretched arm, entwining herself into Boo and Max's joint embrace. She willed herself to not break into tears of joy. A couple of nearby cameras clicked, but she could not have cared less. Jamie finally looked up into Boo's warm eyes.

"Surprised? Good surprised?" Boo asked.

"The best surprise." Jamie sighed her relief at having Boo back in her arms. "When did you get here?"

"We came in last night." Boo motioned with her head to one side of the crowd. Standing next to one of the vans were Isabella and María, now joined by Shon and Chief. They all beamed. "Isabella and María helped me drive the moving truck—they weren't taking any chances."

"Moving truck? Where is it?" Jamie looked around.

"We already unloaded. Shon helped me find a place close to them. I thought, well, it might be a little presumptuous to show up on your doorstep with a moving van. Especially since we haven't officially had our first date yet."

"Well, then, we need to rectify that immediately. Boo Charming, would you do me the honor of going out with me? On a date? Today? Five o'clock, my place?" Jamie raised her eyebrows.

"Me, too," Max chimed in.

Jamie and Boo laughed at Max's enthusiasm.

"Yes, I would love to go on a date with you, Jamie Jordan." Boo kissed Jamie's forehead. "And, Max Jordan, you may join us until your bedtime."

Boo put Max down and pointed him toward their gathered friends and family. Jamie took Boo's face in her hands and kissed her slowly and softly. Twice.

"Just so you know, there will be a lot of kissing on the first date, and all subsequent dates." Jamie winked.

Jamie took Boo's hand as they walked toward the people they loved, to continue the day, together.

Acknowledgments

MY DEEPEST GRATITUDE to Janet James for reading and encouraging, and for putting down her camera long enough to thoroughly edit the manuscript and try to teach me how to be a better writer. My extraordinary beta-team read the manuscript and provided insightful comments and reactions. Thank you to Clare for the running commentary of her thoughts as she read the book (I wish there was a "reader's commentary" version so others could enjoy the comments as much as I did). My appreciation to Beatriz, who translated my poor Spanish into something that made sense. Kristen, thanks for the very explicit suggestions; every romance writer should be so lucky to have a sexologist friend willing to provide comments. Thanks to Paz for the generosity of her time and insights. I am grateful to Anne for years of encouragement, and all of the romance books she passed along. To my mother, who has always supported and encouraged me – I am a very lucky daughter. And, to my loving and lovely partner, Sherry, for going along on this journey.

Please note: The characters and events in this book are fictitious. Please do not take medical or legal advice from this book or any work of fiction. While I do research on topics I write about, I am not trained in the medical field nor am I a lawyer. Although, according to experts, and in my experience, the part about copperheads giving off a faint cucumber odor is true.

Additional acknowledgements, for cover design: EL Bossert; and cover photos: rzoze19/Shutterstock.com (top); Gabriela Palai/Pexels.com (bottom).

About the Author

EL Bossert was raised on a small quiet farm, near a small quiet town in the Midwest, with horses, goats, cats, sometimes chickens, and a large black Newfoundland dog who was occasionally mistaken for a bear. EL currently has a day job as a professor, writing books and articles about positive LGBTQ identity and same-sex relationships. EL enjoys spending time with her partner, hiking, and watching movies with friends.

Read more at https://elbossert.wordpress.com.

Printed in Great Britain
by Amazon